In Sickness & Amnesia

Chrissie Clay

Also by

Brooklyn Bridge Bae

The Truth about Marriage: 8 Principles for Sustaining a Christian Marriage

Virginia is for Lovers: Book 1

Falling for Dez

Virginia is for Lovers: Book 1

So, This is Christmas

Introduction

Hey!

Thanks for reading this book. If you've read other books by me, then welcome back :) if this is your first encounter with me, then welcome! This novel is a quick and sweet romance read (though Dallas may have you thinking otherwise at first, lol). As a warning, this book uses strong language and contains a few explicit scenes. Aside from that, I hope you enjoy Dallas and Shauntay's love story. Please share your thoughts and feelings with me via Instagram (chrissie.clay), TikTok (chrissie_clay), or on Amazon.

Enjoy!

Contents

Playlist

Please enjoy the accompanying playlist.

In Sickness and Amnesia (Spotify)

In Sickness and Amnesia (Apple)

Prologue

FEBRUARY 14, 2022

"See y'all later," Shauntay tells her friends as they disperse from the restaurant. She remote starts her car before tossing her purse in the passenger's seat and getting in.

"Hey, boo," she says, answering the phone.

"Don't 'hey boo' me. It's Valentine's, and I'm here alone because you want to hang out with your girls."

Shauntay laughs. "Now you know I had to take care of my girls," she says, turning onto the street.

"When are you going to take care of me?"

Shauntay smiles before glancing at an SUV in her rearview mirror. "I'm on my way to take care of you now. Just be patient."

"Don't tell me about patience. I'm still waiting for you to file—"

"Don't bring that up. I'll be there soon. This SUV behind me is driving kinda close," she says, glancing in her mirror again.

"Switch lanes."

"I'm not even on the highway yet. I'm driving through downtown."

"Be careful, Tay."

Shauntay turns down Capitol Ave, and as she slows to brake behind the truck in front of her, the SUV behind continues toward her at full speed.

"Shit, I think he's going to hit me!'

"Move out of the way, Tay!"

CRASH!

"Tay?! Tay?!"

Chapter 1: Shauntay Monroe

FEBRUARY 17, 2022

Wake up, Shauntay. Now!

"Daddy?" I mumble. "I don't want to get up yet."

"Go get a doctor!" A voice urges.

"Momma, just press the button to call a nurse," another voice explains.

I open my eyes, but everything is blurry. I close and rub them before opening them again. I try to sit up, but I'm in a lot of pain.

Someone grabs hold of me then. "Thank You, Jesus! My baby is alive!'

"Momma?" I ask. My voice is hoarse. "Momma, where are we?" I ask, my vision slowly becoming restored. "And where's Daddy? I thought I heard his voice."

"The doctor's on the way," a younger voice says.

"Ashantee?" I ask, calling for my older sister.

"Just relax, Tay," she tells me.

An older Black woman in a white jacket enters and raises my bed, causing me to sit up.

"Good morning. I'm Dr. Evans. Can you tell me your full name?" she asks, inspecting my eyes with a flashlight.

"My name is Shauntay Renae Sanford."

From my periphery, I see Momma and Ashantee glance at each other. For the first time, I see a tall, dark-skinned man in the room. He's wearing an orange long-sleeve shirt with baggy jeans. He's staring at me intently, but I don't know why.

"Sanford is our maiden name," Ashantee says.

"Maiden name?" I snicker. "That would mean I'm married," I laugh. No one in the room joins in with me.

"You've been married for eight years," Ashantee informs.

"Married to whom? I don't even wanna get married. And where's Daddy? I thought I heard his voice," I say, examining the room.

Momma, Ashantee, and the man in the orange shirt look at each other before looking at the doctor.

"Do you recognize this man?" Dr. Evans asks, bringing the orange shirt beside me.

"No," I say, becoming concerned. "I have no idea who he is, and what am I doing here?" I ask before coughing. Perhaps I'm straining my voice too much, but I still don't understand why my throat hurts."

"You were in an accident, Mrs. Monroe," Dr. Evans informs. "You were sandwiched between a truck and an SUV."

"What?" I whisper.

"This is your third day in the hospital. You've had an extensive amount of surgery," Ashantee explains. "They just took your feeding tube out earlier this morning."

"You're blessed to be alive," Momma says, tears running down her face.

"I don't remember any of that," I say, incredulously. Then I look at the orange-shirt man again.

"Why are you here? Were you involved in the accident?"

"What do you know about yourself?" Dr. Evans asks.

"My name is Shauntay Sanford. I'm twenty-two, and I'm a senior at Atlanta State University."

A horror-stricken look comes across Momma, Ashantee, and the random man's faces.

"What's going on with her?" Momma asks the doctor.

"Your identification lists your last name as Monroe. According to your date of birth, you're thirty years old. According to your family, this man is your husband."

I close my eyes and shake my head. "That's not right. That can't be true." Opening my eyes, I look at the orange-shirt man who's now sitting beside me on the bed. Worry is written on his face. He has a low cut, high cheekbones, thick eyebrows, and juicy lips. His ear is pierced, and he's muscular, but aside from that, he's a stranger.

"Do you have an inkling about what's going on with her?" Ashantee asks Dr. Evans.

"I'd like to run some more tests before making a formal diagnosis, but I suspect that Mrs. Monroe has retrograde amnesia. In short, she can only remember events up to a certain point in her life, and the point is apparently her senior year of college."

"Then she should remember her husband," Momma says.

"When did you and Mrs. Monroe meet, Mr. Monroe?" Dr. Evans inquires.

"We met and started dating during freshman year of college," he answers.

"They're college sweethearts," Ashantee confirms.

I glance at *Mr. Monroe*. "You're cute and all, but there's no way we're married."

He takes out his camera phone and shows me a picture.

"Is that me?" I ask, astonished. In the picture, I'm wearing a sleeveless, low-cut, white wedding dress. Mr. Monroe has his arm around my waist as we smile and stare into each other's eyes. "I look good! My butt came in pretty nicely," I say, chuckling. Once again, no one laughs.

"Mrs. Monroe—"

"Please call me Shauntay," I say, cutting Dr. Evans off.

"Shauntay, I'm going to order a few more tests to ensure we didn't overlook any brain injury. I'm also going to do a full examination. If the results confirm my suspicions, then we'll diagnose you with retrograde amnesia, and after consulting with you, we'll release you later today. It's interesting that you don't remember your husband, but PTSD after head injuries can affect patients differently." Subconsciously, you may be blocking your husband out, just like the car accident."

"Release her where?" Ashantee asks. "Tay still thinks she's in college living with Momma."

"Her husband is who we'd release her to."

"I'm not comfortable with her going home with him. She doesn't even remember marrying him."

Dr. Evans glances at me before looking at Ashantee. "Shauntay seems mentally stable, and she's currently not showing any signs of incompetency, so I'll leave the decision of whom she goes home with to her."

I stare at my *husband*. "Can you leave the room for a moment?"

Mr. Monroe stands and exits the room without saying anything.

"How do y'all feel about him?" I ask Momma and Ashantee.

Ashantee opens her mouth to speak but bites her lip instead. I know my sister, and it's evident that there's something she's not telling me.

"Dallas has been a great husband to you," Momma answers. "A while back he was out of work because his company filed for bankruptcy and closed, but he found another job, and he's been taking care of everything since."

"Do you trust him?" I ask.

"Yes," Momma answers without a doubt.

"I'll go home with him."

"I think you should go home with Momma," Ashantee objects. "You might have a better chance of healing there."

I stare at Ashantee, and she stares back as if she wants me to read her mind or something. "I'll go home with...Mr. Monroe. Being there may jog my memory."

Ashantee sighs. "Fine. I'll be there when I can to help you get settled in."

Chapter 2: Dallas Monroe

FEBRUARY 17, 2022

Though I'm relieved, Peaches... Shauntay is awake and able to be discharged. I'm surprised she chose to come home with me. Especially when she doesn't even know who I am. Turning out of the hospital's parking deck and onto the street, I can't help but replay the scene I walked in on this morning.

I work night shifts at a warehouse. I got off at five this morning and went home to take a nap before going to the hospital. Ms. Lisa, Shauntay's mom, has been staying with her throughout the night, and after I take a nap, I go to the hospital to relieve her during the day. Getting off the elevator and hearing Ashantee say she needed a doctor in Shauntay's room ASAP sent my heart racing. I thought Shauntay had taken a turn for the worst, but I was grateful to find out that she had woken up. The fact that she can't remember me, though... is a blessing and a curse. Nonetheless, Shauntay's my wife, and I made a vow to take care of her, so that's what I'm going to do.

I called out of work tonight because Dr. Evans said Shauntay's first few days home are going to be vital for her healing and memory restoration. I was instructed to try to get Shauntay back to her routine as much as possible without telling her who she used to be. Dr. Evans said on one hand, some patients' memories return after a while when something familiar triggers them. On the other hand, some patients never regain their memories and become completely new people.

Shauntay thinks she's twenty-two and still in college. We're almost thirty-one; college feels like an eternity ago.

"What's your name again?" Shauntay asks, pulling me from my thoughts.

"Dallas M—"

"Monroe," she finishes. "Do you have a middle name, Dallas Monroe?"

"It's Jerome."

"Jerome?" She snickers. "You said we met at freshmen orientation at Atlanta State University?"

"Yes. I got there late because I kept snoozing my alarm. There was only one open seat left, and it was in the middle row by you. We quietly introduced ourselves to each other while campus police went over safety protocol, and we cracked jokes during the entire orientation."

Shauntay chuckles, causing me to glance at her before returning to the road. I don't know the last time I heard her chuckle, let alone crack a smile around me. A genuine one, at least.

"I hope you don't mind me asking questions, Dallas Jerome, but you are taking me home after only knowing each other for a couple of hours. The least you could do is tell me about yourself." A chuckle escapes from me, and Shauntay glances at me. "Am I usually this funny?"

The smile leaves my face. "You aren't, but you used to be when we first started dating and in the earlier parts of our marriage." Sighing, I try to think about basic details to share about myself. "My birthday is August seventh."

"When's my birthday?"

I glance at her, unsure if she truly doesn't know, or if she's testing me. "Your birthday is April ninth."

"Oh," she says, raising an eyebrow. "You have my birthday memorized? I'm surprised you didn't have to look at a calendar."

I chuckle again. "I do have it on my phone's calendar, but I have your birthday, and our wedding anniversary memorized."

"When is our anniversary?"

"June 28th."

"How long have we been married?"

"This year will make nine."

Shauntay claps, impressed, before a curious expression comes across her face. "You said you have the date in your phone's calendar? Are we rich?"

"What?" I ask, confused.

"You have a camera phone, and it must be high-tech if you can save dates to the calendar. Aren't you worried about your bill going up because you're on the internet?"

I burst out laughing. "I have a smartphone. They became very popular during our sophomore year of college. On a smartphone, you can text, call, take pictures, listen to music, and surf the internet. There's one price for unlimited everything; you don't have to worry about minutes or waiting until nine to make calls."

"That sounds too good to be true," she says, shaking her head. "Do I have a phone?"

"Yes," I answer, still amused. "It was destroyed in the accident, unfortunately. I'll file a claim when we get home and get you a new one."

"Tell me about our college life. Did we start dating right after freshmen orientation?"

"No. We exchanged contact information when orientation ended, but I was too shy to ask you out."

"Really? Why?"

"You were gorgeous," I breathlessly answer as a picture of her from college comes to mind.

Shauntay glances at me. "Were?"

I shift in my seat as I swallow a lump in my throat. "You still are, but back then all of the dudes in our freshman class wanted a shot with you. You were a go-getter. You spoke with authority and carried yourself with confidence. You joined a handful of organizations. You became class president sophomore year when our initial president transferred schools." I can't help but smile at her collegiate achievements. "In my mind, you would've never been interested in a kid from Mechanicsville, so I didn't think I stood a chance with you. Because of that, I never contacted you, despite having your number. When I didn't hear from you, I assumed it was because you realized that you were out of my league."

"But something changed, apparently."

"We ran into each other in the cafe in October. You came up to me and complained about not seeing me around campus. You said you lost the purse that had my number, and you were terrible with names, but you wanted to catch up if I had the time. We sat and talked for about an hour. We laughed, shared how the semester was going, and talked about upcoming classes. That's when we found out that we have similar majors, and we would have two classes together in the spring. We exchanged numbers again, this time actually inputting them into each other's phones, and agreed to keep in touch this time. We did, and I asked you to be my girlfriend before we went home for Thanksgiving break. We've been together ever since."

"That's cute," she gushes. "We have similar majors?"

"You majored in business finance, and I did business marketing."

She gives me a baffled look before a lightbulb goes off. "Momma said your company filed for bankruptcy."

I nod. "Mismanagement of funds by the CFO and others led to the company closing. No one else wanted to hire employees that worked for that company, and I didn't want us to stress about finances, so I took the warehouse job."

"That's a commendable thing to do."

I have to force myself to remain quiet. Memory loss Shauntay thinks it's commendable. Prior, Shauntay thought it was good at first but started looking down on me when she got promoted to a payroll specialist supervisor.

"I can't believe I ran for class president. That doesn't even sound like me."

I scoff. "Do you even know who you've become since then?"

She catches onto the tone of my voice. "No," she answers, staring at the side of my face, "but I hope I'm a good person. Taking note of how my family interacts with you and how nice you are to me, I assume we have a good marriage."

I silently turn into the driveway and press the button to open the garage door. Shauntay unbuckles herself and places her hand on the door's lever.

"I'll come around and get the door for you," I say, killing the engine.

"You're such a gentleman," she says, smiling.

Unable to look her in the face, I get out of the SUV. As I make my way to her side, the weight of my conscience is so heavy it feels like someone dropped an anvil on my head. I grab her medicine and hospital bag out of the back of my SUV before opening her door and helping her into the house.

"This is a beautiful home," she gasps as we enter. "Who designed it?"

"You did," I answer, closing the door behind us. "You bought stuff and told me where you wanted it to go, and I said 'yes, ma'am' because my momma taught me that if your wife is happy, then everything else will fall into place."

"I can't wait to meet your mother...re-meet her, I guess," she says, exploring the living room. "I should've been a designer," she says, walking to the China cabinet that houses our wedding dishes, albums, flutes, and her bouquet. "I look so beautiful," she says, staring at a picture of us.

Joining her, I look at the picture as well. "You have more updated pictures on your phone," I tell her. "It'll probably take some days to get a new one, though."

"Aren't my pictures gone because they're saved to the memory card?"

I smile. It must be nice to still be living in a simpler time of technology. "Everything's saved to the cloud," I explain. She glances out the window, confused, and I chuckle. "The cloud is another term for digital storage. Your phone's data isn't saved to one physical device anymore, but in a cloud so that you can access it in situations like this."

Nodding, she takes the album from the China cabinet and sits on the couch. My phone vibrates before I can sit beside her. From the vibration pattern, I know exactly who it is. "Do you want something to drink?" I offer.

"What do we have?"

"Let me check the fridge," I say, walking into the kitchen. "Hello?" I answer my phone.

"Where you at?" Misty asks.

"My wife got discharged from the hospital today, so I'm home with her."

"For how long? When are you coming here?"

"I don't know," I admit, looking in the fridge. "I'll have to stay with her for a while."

"For a while?" Misty unhappily asks. "I can't imagine Shauntay wants you around right now, or in general, which is why you're always with me."

"Things are different," I say, grabbing a bottle of lemonade.

"What do you mean?"

"She has memory loss. She doesn't remember anything, including us being married...or that our marriage was on the rocks."

"You leaving her should be much easier then. You don't have to worry about tears or anything else, so everything's good."

"It's not that easy. There's still—"

"Listen," Misty cuts me off. "I just put on some new lingerie, and I want you to come take it off."

"I can't do this right now," I say before my phone vibrates. Checking it, I see a picture of Misty in a yellow, lacy, one-piece. "Damn, you do look good."

"Dallas!" Shauntay calls from the living room. "Who's this in this picture with us?"

I return the phone to my ear. "Look, for the time being, Shauntay is depending on me to take care of her. I might not be able to see you as often as I used to."

"What?!" Misty asks. "You don't like her. You don't even love her no more. You don't want to be with her. Y'all were in a loveless marriage when I came along."

"I get all of that, Misty, but she doesn't know any of that. I can't just drop her off at her mother's house and say, 'Take her back.'"

"Yes, you can literally do that. Shauntay has no connection to you except word of mouth."

I exhale; I need to sort out my feelings alone, without any bias. "I'll talk to you later," I say, hanging up the phone.

I pour the lemonade into a glass and return to the living room.

"Here you go, Peaches...I mean Shauntay." I haven't called her Peaches in so long, but the way she's been acting today keeps causing the nickname to slip out.

She raises an eyebrow as she takes the drink from me. "Peaches?" she inquires.

"It's what I call you...used to call you."

"Why?"

Rather than answering, I ask, "How does the drink taste?"

"Do I like lemonade?" she asks.

"Dr. Evans said I shouldn't tell you what you like and don't like so that you can figure it out on your own."

She nods before taking a sip. She scrunches up her face before resting the cup on a coaster on the coffee table. "It's sour," she criticizes.

I chuckle. "You prefer yours sweeter. I gave you some of my lemonade. You went grocery shopping last, and the store must've been out of the one you like, so you just picked some up for me."

"I'm so thoughtful," she says, smiling.

No, you like keeping up appearances, I think, but don't say.

"Who's this standing beside Ashantee, Alana, and me?" she asks, pointing to a picture in the album.

I stare at her, baffled. "You remember Alana?"

Shauntay returns an equally confused look. "Of course, I remember Alana. She's my best friend."

"You met her the same day you met me. How do you remember her?" I ask.

Shauntay shrugs before pointing at the woman in the picture she's inquiring about. "Who's this?"

"That's my cousin. She was one of your bridesmaids."

Nodding, Shauntay flips through the album and stops on a picture of her and her dad, Mr. Chuck. "I thought I heard my dad's voice earlier today in the hospital," she says, glancing at me.

"You might have while you were in and out of consciousness."

"Where is he now?"

"He's... away right now," I answer as delicately as possible.

Shauntay buys the answer. "He is a workaholic. He only takes breaks for his fishing trips. I'm surprised he made time for our wedding."

As I stare at Shauntay while she goes through the album, I can't help but consider Misty's words. This is the perfect time to follow through on the divorce; there won't be any emotional baggage, and alimony was never a factor.

The weight from earlier returns. Am I supposed to tell her that we haven't been happily married for the last two years? Do I tell her that I've had a side chick for the last year and a half? Should I tell her that we haven't made love, let alone held each other or kissed, in the last two years? When am I supposed to tell her the truth about her dad?

Shauntay stops at the picture of us putting cake in each other's face at the wedding and laughs. Hearing her laughter brings a smile to my face. Reminiscing about how we met and started dating reminds me of who we used to be. Would it be manipulative to not tell her how bad things were? Would it be selfish to expect things to go back to the way they used to be in hopes that our once happy marriage could be restored?

"What are we doing for dinner?" Shauntay asks, closing the album.

"Do you have a craving for anything?"

"Some Chinese food."

"Chinese food makes you throw up."

"What?" she asks, in disbelief.

"You used to love it and ate it all the time. When you were eating it spring semester of our senior year, you threw up. You tried it one more time, but after you threw up again, you swore it off."

"Was I pregnant?" she asks before her eyes light up. "Do we have any kids?"

I feel my entire mood change. "No, you weren't pregnant. We waited until marriage to have sex. We also don't have any children," I solemnly answer.

"Do we want children? We've been married for eight years, right? Are we having trouble conceiving?"

My throat tightens. "We talked about having children, but... I guess the timing was off."

She stares at me as if she knows there's more to my story. "I could do some hibachi," she replies, changing the conversation.

"I'll get it and come back," I say, needing some air. I don't have it in me right now to tell her about her father...or our son. I can't put her through that again, let alone reopen those wounds on myself. I walk to the garage before stopping and considering having the food delivered. My phone vibrates, and when I check it, I see another picture from Misty. She's blowing me a kiss in a gray one-piece this time. The message under the picture reads: *You really finna let me take this one off alone too?*

Biting my lip, I return to the living room.

"Don't open the door for anyone," I instruct Shauntay.

"What about Momma and Ashantee?"

"They both have a key," I answer, writing my cell number, as well as Ashantee's and Ms. Lisa's, on a piece of paper. "There's a house phone around the corner. I'll be back," I say, before leaving.

As the garage door opens and I get in my SUV, I reply to Misty.

On the way.

Chapter 3: Shauntay Monroe

FEBRUARY 22, 2022

"Girl, if you had any more flowers in here, you'd have to open your own florist shop," Ashantee teases.

I chuckle. "Who you telling? How did everyone find out about my accident so quickly? I can't imagine you and Momma getting on the phone and calling everyone."

"Tay," Ashantee says, shaking her head. "You've gotta get your phone back. Social media is how everyone keeps in contact nowadays. One of your friends must've made a post, and that's how everyone found out."

"Whatever that means," I say, shaking my head before glancing at my sister's bump. "I still can't believe you're pregnant," I tell her.

She smiles. "Four months to go, and Manny is driving me crazy. You know he wants me to quit my job?" she says, shaking her head.

Oddly enough, I remember my sister's wedding, which took place only one year before mine allegedly did. Ashantee glances at her watch before putting down her glass of water and sighing.

"How have things here been, Tay?" she asks, lowering her voice.

I raise an eyebrow. "It's been fine. My mother-in-law, Ms. Sandra, left yesterday after spending a few days with us. She even cooked for me. She's great."

"And Dallas?" Ashantee inquires, her face concerned.

"He's upstairs sleeping for work."

"No, I mean..." She sighs.

"C'mon, Tee. What is it?"

"Are y'all sleeping together?"

"He sleeps in the guest room. He said he doesn't want to make me feel uncomfortable," I answer before smirking. "Unless you're asking if we're having sex. That's none of your business," I say, smiling.

Tee rolls her eyes. "Ain't nobody asking about your sex life. I mean, is he caring and attentive toward you? Do you feel safe here, or do you want to go home with Momma or come to my house?"

I stare at her, utterly confused. "Dallas has been attentive to all my needs... except my sexual ones, but it has only been five days," I say, chuckling. "It's not like we actually know each other. Aside from that, things have been great. He calls me on the house phone during his work breaks to make sure I'm alright. He took me grocery shopping the other day just so I could get out of the house. Is there something I should know about him?"

Tee sighs. "I didn't want to say this in front of Momma at the hospital, but you and Dallas were going to get a divorce."

"What are you talking about?"

Tee moves closer to me. "You've only told Alana and me..." Ashantee looks into my eyes as she trails off. "I think. Anyway, you've been unhappy at home for the last two years or so."

"That can't be right. Dallas is so nice."

"I know he's a nice guy, but I don't know what went wrong. You always shut down whenever I asked what made y'all seek out a divorce lawyer. In short, you told me that things weren't working out, and you didn't want to be with him anymore."

I know Ashantee would never lie to me, but she's not making any sense. Why would Dallas be caring if he doesn't want to be together? "How does he feel about the divorce?" I ask.

Tee shrugs. "I think he was okay with it. Has he not said a single word about this to you?"

"No. He usually brings up our past rather than filling me in on what's going on in the present," I answer, starting to analyze Dallas' behavior. "He told me where I work, and that I currently have short-term disability leave, so there's no need to rush back. He also told me about our finances. Y'know, what accounts bills come out of and so forth. From what I saw, we're doing pretty well financially, so we couldn't have been having money problems."

"How does he feel about you leaving the house?"

I look at my sister suspiciously. "He told me not to open the door for anyone since I don't remember anyone, but I've never tried to go anywhere. Where would I go?" I ask, chuckling. "I did bring up driving, but we only have one car right now, and he uses it for work. Dallas also said he'd be concerned about me driving alone so soon after being discharged from the hospital, not to mention that I don't really know my way around this neighborhood. He's worried about me getting into another accident."

Tee's smartphone dings, and she rolls her eyes after checking it. "I've gotta get back to work, but I'll make more time to visit you. Sis, you're really smart, so don't take everything at face value. Dallas might be waiting for the right time to remind you about the divorce, so try not to get too comfortable."

"Okay," I say, unsure how to process what she's told me.

As we walk to the front door, Ashantee faces me and sighs. "I forgot you still think you're twenty-two." She bites her lip, looking at me concerned. Taking a deep breath, she shakes her head. "Momma said we need to respect your decision, but I want you to know that you have other options if you want to leave." Tee hugs me and kisses my cheek before going to her car.

I stand in the doorpost, waiting for her to pull off. Ms. Sandra also told me to try to act my actual age as much as I can. I'm trying, but it's hard to go from twenty-two to thirty in five days. A delivery truck pulls up as Tee pulls off.

"Good afternoon," the driver says, walking to me.

"Hey," I say, smiling at him.

He hands me a small package before putting a small electronic notepad in my face. He gives me a puzzled look when I don't move.

"Ma'am, can you sign for the package?"

"Sure, where's the pen?"

The man stifles a laugh. "You use your finger to write on the screen."

I look at him, mystified, before doing as he instructs. Out of habit, I sign my maiden name, but the delivery man doesn't seem to care. He nods at me before returning to his truck.

After locking the door, I head to the living room while reading the box. Based on the sender of the package, this is my new smartphone. Grabbing a pair of scissors, I open the box and power the phone on. Dallas has given me a few lessons on touch screens, though he laughed a lot through them. Dallas claims I've been using touch screen phones since college, but as far as I know, I had a Nokia, and my father did not play about me going over my minutes.

Chuckling, I sit on the couch and begin going through the welcome tutorial. I've been thinking about my dad a lot, but no one wants to talk about him, not even Momma. I'm a daddy's girl, and I want him to know I'm alright. I just wish I knew where he is.

When the time comes, the phone prompts me to sign into "the cloud." There's only one email address and password I remember, so I input it, and I'm elated when it works. A pop-up stating that my data and media are currently being transferred gives me the idea to go to the gallery and see what pictures I have on my phone.

Small gray squares appear in the gallery app, and right before I exit, I see a picture appear. Clicking on it, I see me and a group of women, including Alana and Tee. I smile, realizing that it must be a picture of me with friends. Pictures continue loading in random order. Some in the middle, and some at the top. There isn't a timestamp on any of them, so I have no idea which ones are the most recent. While scrolling, I come across a picture of me and Daddy. I'm hugging him under a banner that says, "Happy Retirement." I smile before looking for more pictures from that day. I see one of him, Momma, Ashantee, and me. Just as I'm about to pass it, something catches my eye. My stomach is poking out in the dress I'm wearing. Not knowing how to zoom in, I hold the phone closer to my face.

"Am I..." I trail off. Perhaps, I'd just gained some weight. I scroll through the gallery and see another picture of Dallas kissing my stomach. Gasping, I keep scrolling, looking to see a picture of the baby.

Why would Dallas tell me we didn't have kids if I was pregnant?

I get to the bottom of the gallery, and I see pictures of me. I'm alone, and I have a flat stomach again.

Ashantee's words begging me to act my age replay in my mind as I head to the staircase. I want to remember, but I can't.

Was our child in the car with me during the accident? Then I gasp. *Was Daddy in the car with me too? Am I the only survivor of the accident?*

Though I'm still healing from the surgeries I've had, I race up the steps, and bang on the guestroom door.

"Dallas!" I say, as tears fall down my face. "Dallas, open up! Can I come in?"

Chapter 4: Dallas Monroe

FEBRUARY 22, 2022

"Dallas!"

"Peaches?" I mumble, still half asleep.

"Can I come in?!"

I jump out of bed then. "What's wrong, Peaches?" I ask, rushing to the door.

She looks at me, unable to speak with tears in her eyes. Scenarios start racing through my mind.

"Did something happen to you?" I ask, grabbing hold of her. "I never lock the door in case you need me. Why didn't you come in?"

"My phone got delivered," she finally says.

"Did the delivery driver do something to you?" I ask, glancing out the guest room window.

She shakes her head before taking a deep breath. "I'm sorry to wake you up from your nap."

"You don't have to apologize for that," I say, letting her go and walking to the bed.

"What happened to my dad?" she asks, following me. I try to quickly think of an excuse, but Shauntay says, "And don't lie to me, Dallas. Yesterday you said you'd tell me the truth about anything I asked." She shows me a picture of her and Mr. Chuck from his retirement party.

I exhale heavily before sitting on the bed. "Shauntay, your father died two years ago."

Her arms drop, and she leans forward as if all of the air has been knocked out of her. I catch her and sit her on my lap.

"What do you mean he died?" she asks, barely above a whisper. "I heard his voice in the hospital," she says, looking into my eyes. "I heard him, and you said I might've."

"I was alluding to your near-death experience. I thought you might've seen him as..." I can't finish my sentence.

"How did he die?"

"He had a heart attack a couple of months after his retirement party."

Shauntay takes a deep breath, and I bury her face in my chest, already knowing what's about to come next. She wails into my chest while wrapping her arms around me. I hold her, like I did when he first died and the months after. Shauntay grieved hard for her father, but I can't blame her. He'd been her role model her entire life. Most daughters confide in their mothers. Shauntay was a daddy's girl through and through. She told him everything. She talked to him all the time, and after we moved into our own place, she saw him at least four times a week.

I rub her back as she continues crying. "I'm so sorry you have to go through this again," I say, surprised at my own voice breaking. "Your dad was the only father I had," I say as tears fall from my eyes too. "I learned so much from him," I continue, reminiscing on the ten years I spent with him. Her crying slows, so I continue talking. "He taught me how to do tire and oil changes," I say, smiling. "He always said, 'Ain't no man finna take my daughter anywhere and get stranded,'" I say, chuckling. "He took me on my first fishing trip too."

"Daddy loved fishing," Shauntay whispers. "So, Momma lives in that house all alone now?" she asks, looking into my eyes.

"You asked her to move in with us, and Ashantee asked her to move in with her. Your mother refused, saying, no one will get her out of the house she and your dad worked hard to get."

"Sounds like Momma," Shauntay mumbles, picking up her phone again. She scrolls through some pictures before her eyes widen. "Was I pregnant?" she asks, showing me the phone's screen.

A lump forms in my throat as I look away from her.

"Dallas," she calls.

"Yes, you were."

"Where's our baby, then? Was the baby in the car with me during the accident? Did the child die?" She frantically asks. Glancing at her, I can tell hundreds of thoughts are racing through her head. "I was pregnant with *our* child, right?"

"Yes, he was our son," I answer, looking into her eyes. "You took your father's death really hard. You fainted at the burial site. I was talking to some of your relatives and didn't make it to you in time. Your fall left you unconscious, and by the time we went to the hospital, they said you were stable... but our son died due to the lapse in oxygen."

Shauntay weeps into my chest. I hold her again, but this time I have to rest my head on her because I can't keep from crying. "The doctors did an emergency C-section to try to save him, but he was two months early. Between that and the lack of oxygen...he was a stillborn," I say, as a picture of our son's lifeless body flashes into my mind.

"I'm so sorry, Dallas," Shauntay says between breaths. "I'm sorry that happened."

"Why are you apologizing?" I ask, lifting her head so I can look into her eyes.

"It's my fault our son's dead," she tearfully responds.

My face softens as her words register. She's never told me she felt responsible for Daniel's death before, and I wonder if that's what led to our separation in the first place. "You don't ever have to apologize to me for that," I sincerely say. "That was not your fault." She looks away, but I turn her face back to mine. "That wasn't your fault, Peaches. Sometimes bad things just happen," I tell her.

Nodding, she wipes my face before gasping. "I remember," she whispers.

"You remember what?"

"We all went out to eat. Daddy said he wasn't feeling well... that he hadn't been feeling well all day. He collapsed in the restaurant's parking lot," Shauntay whispers before looking into my eyes. "I remember the funeral too. I remember how I felt waking up in the hospital and hearing the doctor tell me that...Daniel?" she asks. I nod. "I remember hearing that Daniel didn't make it. Was that our only chance at having a baby?"

"You don't remember anything else? Anything about us?" I ask. She shakes her head, and I look away. "No, that wasn't our only chance at having a baby."

"Did we not want to try again?"

I silently ponder a response. I know I said I'd tell her the truth about everything, but how do I tell the truth without making her sound like a villain? The truth is Shauntay grieved for about three months, and then she wouldn't touch me. She wanted nothing to do with me. Some days she couldn't even look at me. I asked why, and even suggested therapy, but she wasn't interested in reconciliation. I met Misty shortly after that.

"I got the warehouse job after all that happened. You'd just be getting home by the time I had to leave, and our schedules just never seemed to make the time to try again," I say, sugarcoating the truth to the best of my ability. I don't want her to think she was a terrible person previously because she wasn't. Up until her father's death, Shauntay had been the perfect wife, even with the few arguments we had.

Now calmer, Shauntay gets off me and looks around the room.

"Something wrong?" I ask.

She shakes her head. "I've never been in here before, so I wanted to see why you prefer sleeping in here instead of our room." I open my mouth to offer the lie that I'm sleeping in here because she doesn't remember me, but she speaks before I do. "Can you help me finish setting up my phone? I did a little bit."

Nodding, I pick up the phone that's beside me on the bed. All of her information hasn't downloaded from the cloud because she isn't connected to Wi-Fi, and it'll use too much data to download without it. I connect her to the Wi-Fi as she glances at me. I look up, and she turns around, embarrassed.

Was she checking me out?

"I didn't mean to stare," she says, walking to the window. "Do you always sleep in your boxers, or have you run out of PJs but you're too scared to come into our room?"

"I usually sleep like this," I answer.

She faces me, biting her lip. I clear my throat, and she smiles awkwardly. "If my nickname is Peaches, why do you have a peach tattoo on your chest?"

"Because you wanted us to get matching tattoos," I answer, as her phone starts vibrating in my hand. All of her missed notifications begin pouring in now.

"I don't have a tattoo," Shauntay argues, returning to me.

"You have a tattoo on your upper thigh. You put it there to hide it from your parents... though you squealed about it to your dad a few months later," I say, chuckling as her text messages begin coming through.

Shauntay lifts her dress, causing me to lick my lips. I never stopped being attracted to her. Even now as the sun illuminates her brown skin, and she cluelessly looks for her tattoo, I find her attractive. She's been wearing her hair in an afro puff since her discharge, but that doesn't take away from her beauty. I love when she wears dresses, and that's why she has a closet full of them now. This pink bodycon dress she's wearing is turning me on, even more now that she's flashing me.

"I guess I do have a peach tattoo," she says, dropping her dress.

Though I'm enticed, I recognize a larger issue. "Shauntay, you've been home for five days, and you haven't seen your tattoo?" I ask. She shrugs. "What about when you shower?" Which I know she does because she frequently forgets where the linen closet is, and I have to show her so she can get a new towel and washcloth. Shauntay shrugs again, and I become alarmed.

"Aside from my mom, do you remember any other visitors you've had?"

"Ashantee came to see me today."

"What about our friends?"

"What friends?" she cluelessly asks.

"Our friends from college that came three days ago. They spent almost an entire day with us."

Shauntay shakes her head. "Only Ms. Sandra and Tee have visited."

"That's concerning. I'm going to call your doctor and schedule a follow-up appointment," I tell her.

"Okay," she shrugs. "How's it going with the phone?"

Glancing down, I see that her contacts are currently being registered, but her phone keeps vibrating with messages from an unsaved number. I click on the thread, and my heart drops while reading the most recent message.

Baby, are you okay? Call me now!

Who the hell is this calling my wife baby?

"I'm going to start packing your lunch," Shauntay announces as she leaves.

"Okay," I mumble, scrolling up on the message thread.

This has to be a wrong number. There's no way that she was with another man.

But that's when I see it. The time and location of meetups. The messages about how good last night was, and how she can't wait to do it again. As I keep scrolling, I find pictures of them. Some of Shauntay sitting on his lap and kissing him. Some with him kissing her cheek. Some of them are just smiling while out to eat. My heart pounds so loud I hear it in my ears. There's no way in hell she's cheating on me.

Zooming in on the picture, I realize that I recognize the man. He's one of her coworkers that I met at her job's Christmas party a while back. If memory serves correctly, it was the Christmas party of the year her father died. I wanted to accompany her so that she wouldn't be alone, but thinking back, she really didn't care to have me there. Our intimacy had since plummeted, but I still wanted to be there for her because our marriage was more than sex. But by that time, she wouldn't even hold my hand, so how did she start having an affair with this man?

Dropping her phone, I head to the door to confront her, but I stop. There's no point. If she doesn't remember me or our friends, then there's no way she remembers that nigga.

I can't get those pictures of the two of them out of my mind though. I pace back and forth in the room before stopping in front of the wall and punching it. Shauntay has always had a high sex drive, so I should've known better than to think she was being abstinent for the last two years. For six months I waited for her to return to normal, or find a new normal, meanwhile she was getting piped down by some pencil pusher? I punch the wall again.

The first time I slept with Misty, I felt so bad that I cried in the car before returning home. It took months for me to get used to cheating. Meanwhile, she was doing it like it was no big deal? I punch the wall again. This time, not only do I create a hole, but I also draw back my fist with blood. I guess I'm in pain, but the heartbreak is too strong for me to feel anything else.

I wash my hands in the bathroom before throwing on some work clothes and heading downstairs.

"You're leaving kinda early, aren't you?" Shauntay says, as I walk past her in the kitchen.

"I got called in," I lie.

"What about your lunch?"

"I'll grab a bite to eat," I say, going into the garage and slamming the door behind me.

I hardly make it out of the neighborhood before I call Ashantee.

"Hey. Is everything okay with Shauntay?" Ashantee asks.

"Your sister was cheating on me?"

Ashantee remains silent.

"Did you know?" I ask.

"I knew a little something."

"Are you kiddin' me, Ashantee?! You knew Shauntay was cheating on me, and you ain't have the balls to tell me? You didn't even try to talk her out of it?"

"Let's be fair, Dallas, you're cheating too!"

Now I'm silent.

"You've had a side chick for a while now. How dumb do you think my sister is? What's dumb is the fact that y'all were both cheating on each other yet tiptoed around a divorce."

"Who is this nigga anyhow?"

"I don't know," Ashantee sighs. "Even if I did, I still wouldn't tell you. I don't need you causing a scene, and you know you got a mean streak."

I spent one night in jail during college for fighting a dude that wouldn't take no for an answer from Shauntay, and now Ashantee forever labels me as having a mean streak.

"It sounds like you're driving. Where are you going?" Ashantee asks.

"I'm going to work."

"This early?" she scoffs. "You're probably on your way to that slut's place right now."

Sucking my teeth, I hang up the phone. Though I am on my way to Misty's apartment, I consider heading downtown and pulling up to Shauntay's job. If my suspicion is right and that clown does work with her, then I'd be going to jail again.

Sighing, I shake my head and continue to Misty's apartment. I'm not fighting anyone for that ...I can't even fix my mouth to call Shauntay out her name. I park, get out, and walk to Misty's door. I unlock it without even giving her a head's-up.

"I didn't think you were coming over here today," she says, glancing from the TV to me. I look around her apartment, and she gives me a confused face. "What you lookin' for?" she asks, returning to the TV.

"I just found out Shauntay's been cheating on me."

Misty turns up her nose at me. "I could've told you that a long time ago. You really think a married woman is going to go two years without sex?"

"How did I not notice?" I ask, banging my hands on the counter. "How could she have not left a single clue?"

"Calm down, babe," Misty says, approaching me. "It sounds like you found a reason for your divorce. Use this as ammunition and leave that woman in the past."

Exhaling, I begin calming down. "I just can't believe that backstabbing... I can't believe she'd let somebody else tap what's supposed to be mine."

"I got yours right here," Misty says, putting her hair in a ponytail. "And no one's tapped it since your last visit," she says, dropping to her knees and unbuckling my pants.

***

"Damn, Dallas. You alright tonight?" one of my coworkers asks.

"I'm fine."

"You done did half of tonight's tasks, and it's only been four hours. You need to go home and work off some sexual tension?"

"Leave me alone, bruh," I say, heading to the office to clock out for lunch.

After doing so, I go to my locker and take my phone out. This is the time I usually call Shauntay to check on her, but tonight, I couldn't care less what's going on with her. I should've deleted the thread so she wouldn't try to reach out to him. The number isn't saved, so she would've just thought he was a stranger if he tried to contact her again. I should've pulled up to her office like I wanted.

Closing my locker, I walk to the break room trying to understand why I care so much about what and who she was doing. I have my own affair going on, so hers shouldn't bother me. But it does. The pain burns a hole in my chest as if someone placed a branding iron on it. The pictures of her and that man flash through my mind again. I can't believe she'd do that.

Not the woman who waited until marriage for sex. Not the woman who said she couldn't even lie down with another man unless she loved him. That couldn't be her in those pictures.

Trying to distract myself, I decide to check my missed notifications and see an email from Justin Campbell, a divorce lawyer Shauntay and I reached out to last month. Opening the email, I read his message inquiring about whether or not Shauntay and I want to follow through with the divorce. Tears fall from my eyes as I reread the email. How could I allow my marriage to reach this all-time low? How am I supposed to say goodbye to the woman I wanted to do everything with?

Chapter 5: Shauntay Monroe

MARCH 4, 2022

Turning off *Murder, She Wrote*, I grab my phone and head to the kitchen. It's been quiet around the house for the last week or so, and I'm not sure why. Dallas is still polite to me, but he's not as engaging as he was when I first came home. Maybe this is why Ashantee told me not to get comfortable.

Opening the fridge, I see the chicken for tomorrow's dinner seasoned and waiting to be cooked. I also see Dallas' lunchbox. He's been leaving without it lately, claiming he'll "grab something on the way." He's also been leaving earlier than expected, but he said it had to do with a schedule change. Whatever the reason for his distance, he still has been taking care of things that I need. For instance, he filed a claim with our insurance for my totaled car before I even left the hospital. Because of his promptness, last Friday I was able to get a new vehicle for next to nothing with the check issued by the insurance company. I got a silver RAV4. It's my first SUV, and I was happy to drive it off the lot, but Dallas is still apprehensive about me driving alone. When he's available, he accompanies me as I explore the neighborhood we live in. Sometimes he even quizzes me to see if I can make it to church or my mom's house and back home without any directions.

I take the chicken out of the fridge and decide to cook it now. I quickly became accustomed to Dallas' late phone calls to check on me while he was at work. Now that he's stopped, I'm left feeling...abandoned. Nonetheless, one of the reasons I decided to come home with Dallas is to see if our marriage, and my memories, can be restored, so I'm not going to give up, despite the funk he's been in.

As I hit shuffle on a playlist, I devise a plan. After cooking, I'm going to get dolled up, and surprise Dallas at work with his lunch. Glancing at the clock, I realize I don't have much time, so instead of baking the chicken, I fry it. I pack a salad for a side, and the cookies I baked earlier for dessert. After grabbing a bottle of lemonade for him and a bottle of water for me, I race upstairs to get myself together.

***

I silently thank the Lord as I park in the warehouse's parking lot. I thought I forgot the place he worked, but I see his SUV in the parking lot and know I'm at the right spot. Dallas and my doctor were worried about me not being able to form new memories, but after careful observation, they wrote it off as a one-time incident. I've been able to remember recent day-to-day events and people I re-meet.

I pull down the visor and give myself a quick look-over. Ashantee took me to the spa earlier, and I asked for a silk press. I'm happy my curls are still bouncy. I didn't want to do a full face of makeup, so I put on eyeshadow, mascara, and lip gloss... though I probably could've put on lipstick because it's not like Dallas and I kiss... or do anything else. I'm also wearing a short-sleeve maxi dress with flats and a jeans jacket. Thankfully, it's not too cold tonight. I grab the tote I packed, get out of the SUV, and enter the building.

I enter the front office and ring the bell at the counter. A man appears a short while later. He smiles when he sees me.

"Hey. What's a cutie like you doing here at this time of night?"

I chuckle. "Hey, I'm Shauntay Sand... Monroe. I'm here to see my husband, Dallas. I brought him something to eat. Could you get him for me?"

The man's face deflates at the mention of Dallas. "I can take the food to him, but I'm not sure if I can call him away from the back right now."

Another man walks in with his face glued to a clipboard. "What are you doing back here?" he asks the man who was helping me.

"This woman rang the bell."

The older man looks at me, and his eyes widen. "Shauntay?"

I smile awkwardly. "Hey. Do I know you?"

The man nods his head. "Dallas mentioned you had memory loss. I'm his supervisor, Darnell. What are you doing here?"

"I brought him some food."

Darnell looks at me suspiciously before turning to the other man. "Tell Dallas to come here." The man leaves, and Darnell faces me again. "How have you been? I haven't seen you in a while."

"Did I used to stop by often?"

Darnell tilts his head from left to right. "Occasionally. Whether to say hi, or to drop off Dallas' lunch."

I smile. "Then what I'm doing isn't out of the ordinary."

"No, but it's been almost two years since you've done this."

Everything keeps circling back to two years ago. Did I have a mental breakdown when Daddy died or something?

"You need me, Darnell?" Dallas asks, walking into the office. Darnell nods in my direction, and when Dallas faces me, he becomes awestruck. "Shauntay," he finally says, "What are you doing here?"

"I know I'm a little early, but I brought you some dinner...I guess it's lunch for you...I brought some food and wanted to see if you'd want to eat together."

Dallas continues staring at me, though I'm now unsure if it's because of how I look or because of what I suggested.

"Go ahead," Darnell permits. "I'll fix your timecard."

"Okay," Dallas says, walking from behind the counter. "I need to wash up. Do you remember where the break room is?"

I put a hand on my hip and look at him. "I barely remember who you are; do you think I remember where the breakroom is?"

He chuckles, catching me off guard. "Just follow me. How did you get here?"

"GPS."

"That was dangerous, but I'm glad you made it here safely."

We stop at a door, and Dallas asks me to wait outside. I hear water running for a while before there's silence.

I give him a confused look when he exits with a completely clean face and hands. "Y'all got towels and stuff in there?"

"Yes. We have full bathrooms, in case anyone needs to take a shower after their shift."

I nod as we continue walking down an orange-lit hallway. We stop at another door, and after walking through it, I'm surprised how comfortable and welcoming it is for a warehouse. There are tile floors, vending machines, two TVs, two couches, a refrigerator, and tables with cushioned chairs.

"I appreciate you bringing me something to eat, but you didn't have to go out of your way to do that," he says, taking the tote from me and resting it on a table.

"I couldn't sleep anyway, and since you're always grabbing a bite to eat, I figured you'd like a home-cooked meal. Sit down, and I'll serve you."

Dallas looks confused but does as I instruct anyway. While I'm unpacking the bag, I catch him checking me out and licking his lips.

"The chicken smells so good," he says, when everything is on the table.

"Let's hope it tastes that way too," I say, bringing a piece to my mouth.

As we eat, he compliments my hair and apologizes for not noticing it before he left the house today. Blushing, I thank him before showing him my nails since I also got a manicure and pedicure.

"What made you go with green?" he asks, taking my hand in his. It's the first time he's touched me since I've been home, not including the day he held me when I found out my father died.

"I'm not sure," I say, shrugging. "Something about it drew me in."

"Green is my favorite color," he says, looking into my eyes.

Chuckling, I look away. "How's work going?"

"It's been fine," he answers, surprised at the change of topic.

"You've been leaving early the last few days, and I've been wondering if I did something wrong," I say, returning to his eyes. "Did I offend you...or is it something else?"

He places my hand on the table and reaches for his lemonade, though he doesn't drink it. "You haven't offended me or done anything wrong," he finally answers.

"I've been working on rebuilding every part of my life. I've been reconnecting with my sister and her husband, talking to Momma and accepting that Daddy's dead, and I've been hanging out with your mom too. But I feel like the only part of my life that hasn't been rekindled is my relationship with you." I give him a chance to say something, but he remains silent. "I'd like to start working on it, and building some intimacy between us," I say, putting my hand on his. He looks at me then. "Unless you don't want to. Unless you want us to go our separate ways."

"N-no... It's not that. I don't want to leave you when you're so vulnerable. I made a vow to stick by you, so I need to be there for you."

I lean across the table to caress his cheek. "If there wasn't a vow, would you want to leave? Be honest with me."

He sighs, and I let him go. "Honestly, I don't know, Shauntay. A lot has happened between us and..." He shakes his head. "I don't know."

"I can't apologize for mistakes that I don't even know I made. Why don't I give you some time to think about what you want to do when it comes to us?"

"Okay," he says, reaching for the cookies. "These are delicious. Where did you get them?"

"I baked them when Ashantee and I got back from the spa," I admit. "I've been dabbling in the kitchen, so I'm glad you like it."

"You've always been a good cook, but I didn't know you could bake too."

"I googled a recipe. 500 results generated. Where was that when we had to use *Ask Jeeves* for our research papers?"

Dallas does a gut-wrenching laugh, causing me to smile. "Peach...Shauntay, *Ask Jeeves* isn't even a thing anymore. It's just *Ask.com*. Most people just google things now."

"You can call me Peaches if you like," I say, looking at him.

We stare into each other's eyes for a while before he says, "I call you Peaches because you're my Georgia peach."

"Then why do you say Peaches instead of Peach?"

He starts blushing then. "Because you have some juicy peaches," he whispers, glancing at my breasts before leaning to the side to catch a glimpse of my butt.

I hide behind my hands. "You're corny," I say, smiling from ear to ear.

The breakroom door swings open, and Darnell enters. "Dallas, I told you to take a break, not the rest of the night off. Hurry up."

I apologetically face Darnell. "My bad. I didn't mean to keep him this long." I look at Dallas then. "I'll see you when you get home."

"Okay."

"I'll have breakfast waiting for you," I say, packing the items back in the bag.

"I'd like that," he says, smiling.

"What time will you be home?"

"Around six."

"Oh," I say, surprised. "Earlier than usual. Nice."

Picking the tote up, I smile at Darnell before walking out of the room.

"Earlier than usual," Darnell repeats as the door closes behind me. "You've been getting off at five. What time have you been getting home?"

I stop in the hallway to listen for Dallas' reply.

"Around seven or eight."

"Where have you been going?"

"I don't want to talk about it," Dallas answers.

My heart races as I speed down the hallway to the exit. The fact that Dallas and I were planning to get a divorce has haunted me every day since Ashantee told me about it. As I get in my vehicle and put my address in the GPS, I wonder if I'm doing the right thing by trying to work on our marriage. Perhaps, I should let this relationship go and follow through with the divorce. I don't even know this man. I should leave and move back in with Momma.

Chapter 6: Dallas Monroe

MARCH 11, 2022

"Dallas!"

I mute the TV, unsure if I hear someone calling my name, or if I'm imagining things.

"Dallas!" I hear, followed by knocking on the wall.

I get out of bed and quickly make my way into the master bedroom. I hear the shower running, so I enter the en suite bathroom. Though it's steamy, I keep my head down, so I don't accidentally peek at the frameless glass shower door.

"You called, Shauntay?"

Opening the door and sticking her head out, she says, "Sorry to bother you, but I forgot to grab a towel and washcloth. Could you get them for me?"

I raise an eyebrow. "Do you still remember where the linen closet is?"

She chuckles. "Yes. What I don't remember is why we don't keep towels in here for us. It doesn't even matter because when I get out, I'm bringing all the cute towels in here."

Chuckling, I leave to retrieve the towels for her and return. "Here you are," I say, hanging the towel on the rack and facing away from the shower door as I extend the washcloth toward it.

The door opens, Shauntay takes the washcloth, but I don't hear the door close. When I face the shower, I see Shauntay looking at me nervously.

"Can you...get my back?" she asks, her tone gentle and sweet.

I stare into her eyes, positive I didn't hear her correctly. "If you want me to," I finally answer.

Nodding, she takes the washcloth and soaps it up. The condensation prevents me from seeing clearly, but I assume she's washing the front of her body. A little while later, she opens the shower door wider and offers me the washcloth. I take it from her as I move closer.

I start at her neck before moving to her shoulders and upper back. As my hand moves lower, I notice the curve leading to her butt. I have to stop myself from drooling, and getting hard, but damn, my wife has a beautiful body. I get her waist and finally her butt.

"I'll take that from you now," Shauntay says, turning slightly so she can face me. She has one arm across her chest, concealing some of her breasts, while stretching for the washcloth with her free hand.

I give her the washcloth and wait to see if she'll ask me to leave, but she doesn't. I watch her wash her legs before she rinses and wrings out her washcloth as the water washes the soap from her body. The more I stare, the more I want to take off my clothes and join her. Shauntay turns away from me to hang the washcloth on the rack, giving me a full view of her backside. Though I'm loving every second of this show, something catches my eye.

"When did you get that?" I ask.

"Get what?"

"This right here," I say, touching her upper right shoulder.

"I don't know what you're talking about."

I grab a handheld mirror from the bathroom vanity as Shauntay turns off the water and wraps herself in a towel. I position the mirror so she can see the butterfly tattoo in the corner on her right shoulder.

"I dunno," she says, scrutinizing the tattoo. "I don't even remember this one," she says, pointing to the peach tattoo on her thigh.

"Nah, I know that one because we both got peach tattoos that day," I remind her. "But I don't recall you mentioning that butterfly one."

Shauntay shrugs while walking to the bathroom counter. "Does it mean something to you?" She nonchalantly asks.

I tell myself to remain calm, though I feel my blood boiling. I haven't seen my wife's body in two years, and the first time I do, I find a tattoo that she never told me about. I'm equally hurt and pissed.

"Maybe I got it when I was out with my friends on a girls' trip or something, and I forgot to tell you," Shauntay says, drying herself off.

Leaving the bathroom, I mumble, "Or maybe you got it while you were with that other nigga."

The doorbell rings before I can make it back to the guest room. Sighing, I go downstairs to see who it is.

"Hey, Alana," I say, opening the door for Shauntay's best friend.

"Hey, Dallas," she smiles.

"Shauntay's almost been home for a month, and you wait until now to visit her?" I ask, motioning for Alana to enter the house.

She rolls her eyes as she walks past me. "You know I don't like crowds. I was not going to visit while y'all had all those other people in the house. But I sent flowers, and I've been talking to Tay every day since she's gotten her phone back."

I follow Alana to the kitchen. "What were y'all doing downtown the night of the accident?" I ask her.

"We went out for margaritas with some other girls. Valentine's Day isn't all about romantic love, you know."

"But why would Shauntay go down Capitol Ave? That's a roundabout way to get to our house."

Alana raises an eyebrow before grabbing a glass from the cabinet. "Where is Tay?"

"She just got out of the shower. I'll tell her you're here," I say, heading to the staircase. I stop and face Alana instead. "Did you know she has a tattoo?"

Alana gives me a baffled look. "You mean the one y'all got in college?"

"No. A butterfly tattoo on her back."

Alana rests the glass on the counter before awkwardly looking around the kitchen. "I may have known a little something about it," she whispers.

"Did you also know she was cheating on me?"

Alana rolls her eyes and drops her purse on the counter. "Yes."

"And you didn't tell me?"

Alana shrugs. "I thought about telling you, but you'd never believe me, so I kept quiet."

"That's trifling."

Alana scoffs. "What's trifling is you getting with Shauntay when you know I've wanted you since we met freshman year."

"Not this again," I say, turning to leave.

Alana grabs my arm, though. "What's trifling is that you had the nerve to have an affair with some random chick when you have me right here."

"Like I've been telling you since college, I'm not interested in you. I only want Shauntay."

"Obviously not. That's why you're running around behind her back with some hoe."

Chapter 7: Shauntay Monroe

MARCH 11, 2022

Our slanted staircase is carpeted, so Dallas and Alana don't hear me descending. I freeze right before I make it to the last two steps. Did I hear Alana correctly? I've had my suspicions, but did she just admit that Dallas is cheating on me? There's a thin wall separating the kitchen from the staircase, so I peep around it to get a better look into the kitchen.

"Had we just gotten together in college, then you wouldn't be in this predicament. You never would've felt neglected or felt the need to step out on your wife," Alana says, pushing her breasts against Dallas' chest. "I've never stopped wanting you."

Dallas backs away from her. "You're married. Go home to your husband."

"I don't want him!" she disgustedly replies. "I'm only with him for his money. We all know that was a marriage of convenience."

"Whatever it is, you need to go work it out with him. I don't want you here."

"One taste won't hurt," she says, rubbing his arm.

"Go home, Alana," Dallas says, moving to the other side of the kitchen. "I don't know how Shauntay became friends with you. I wish she would see you for who you truly are."

"So, you had a shot with her, but you don't think I had the right to become her friend?" Alana laughs. "We all know how Shauntay was in college, trusting and always looking for the best in everybody. She was also very ambitious...no wonder she got promoted at work so quickly." Dallas approaches Alana like he wants to hit her but exhales and leans on the island instead. "Just kidding. She got the promotion on merit alone. But Shauntay had her hands in a little of everything, and because of that, she was someone who could connect me to the right people. Why wouldn't I gravitate to someone like that?"

"Of course you would, you leech."

"I could show you how much of a leech I am," Alana chuckles.

"Get out of my house."

"Nope," Alana says, picking up a glass. "I came to spend time with Shauntay, and I'm not leaving until I do."

Taking a deep breath, I start humming, as if I'm only now descending the steps. "Hey, Alana," I say, entering the kitchen. "When did you get here?"

"Not too long ago," she answers, smiling at me. "You've healed up pretty nicely."

"Thanks," I say before facing Dallas. "You aren't going to take a nap?"

He gives me a suspicious look before heading to the steps. "A nap won't hurt."

"I'll see you when you get up," I say, smiling.

He smiles at me before leaving.

"Girl," Alana says, placing the glass in my hand. "Make me a drink while I fill you in on what's been going on."

"You want anything specific?" I ask.

"You know our usual: mango margaritas," Alana answers before talking about someone named Kaseem. I drown her out while grabbing a glass for myself.

I pour the mix into both of our glasses and add some tequila before opening the fridge to look for some juice. Aside from lemonade, we have tropical punch and berry punch. I grab the tropical one since it'll go better with the mango mix. As I pour the juice into our glasses, an alarm goes off in the depths of my mind. I don't know what it's for, so I ignore it.

Alana has not stopped talking, nor has she realized that I'm not paying attention to her story. I'm livid, but I don't know how to express it. No prior memories of Dallas and me have returned, so though I'm mentally pissed about what I heard, emotionally I'm removed from the news of his affair. What's fueling my rage is the fact that my so-called best friend has been harboring feelings for my husband. Though I remember Alana and the fact that we're best friends, I don't remember everything about her. For instance, I don't remember seeing her the day of my accident. I don't remember her being in my wedding because I don't remember my wedding, but I also don't remember the time in college when we were allegedly suitemates. I do remember that she's married and that she doesn't want any kids.

"Girl, stop stirring those drinks and serve them already," Alana orders.

I drop the spoon in the sink before giving her a glass. Alana drinks a third of the glass before placing it on the counter.

"This has a weird taste to it. What did you use?"

I sip my glass before answering. "Mine tastes fine. I used the mango margarita mix, tequila, and tropical punch."

Alana's eyes widen. "Tropical punch? What's in the punch, Shauntay?"

I give Alana a baffled look before going to the fridge to retrieve the juice box. "Guava, mango, pineapple—"

"Pineapple?!" Alana shrieks. "I am allergic to pineapple, Shauntay. You know this!" Alana says, trying to even her breathing.

"You're what?" I ask, placing my glass down and walking over to her.

"I'm gravely allergic to pineapple," she says, digging through her purse. "I'm getting dizzy, Tay. Call an ambulance. Now!"

"Okay, but I don't have my phone. I left it upstairs. Dallas will get it," I say, cupping my mouth and facing the staircase. "Dallas!"

Alana grabs my hand and gives me her purse. "Use...my phone," she barely gets out.

I retrieve her phone in no time. "What's your password?"

Alana leans against the wall, panic in her eyes. "You don't remember my password? You're the only person in the world who knows my code, and you're telling me you don't remember it?"

I shrug, and Alana's eyes fill up with tears. "Dallas!" she calls.

Dallas races down the stairs in a matter of seconds. "What's wrong?" he asks, examining me.

"Shauntay just gave me pineapple juice," Alana says, sliding down the wall.

"I gave you tropical punch," I correct.

"She's allergic to pineapple," Dallas says, looking at me, alarmed.

I raise an eyebrow. "Does everybody know about her allergy? Did I know about her allergy?"

Dallas faces Alana. "Do you have an EpiPen?"

"Yes, yes! There's one in my purse."

Dallas looks through the purse as Alana lies on the floor. "It has to be injected into your thigh," Dallas says, walking to Alana. She lifts up her dress.

"Uh-uh," I say, stepping in front of Dallas. "Give me that. You're a married man. You're not going up another woman's dress; you haven't even been up my dress."

"This is... not the time...for that," Alana says.

"Why don't you call for an ambulance?" I tell Dallas.

"Y'all haven't even called 9-1-1 yet?" He hysterically asks, taking his phone out of his pocket.

Ignoring him, I walk over to Alana. "You don't look so well. Your cheeks are puffy. Can you breathe?" Alana closes her eyes and leans her head back. I roll my eyes. "You don't have to be so dramatic." I quickly read how to use the device before launching it into her thigh.

She groans as I hold the device in place for the required amount of time.

"Just relax, Alana," Dallas says, joining us. "Help is on the way."

I glance at him and smile. Confused, he walks to the door. I stay by Alana's side and silently wait with her. She's breathing, but she doesn't say much. When the paramedics arrive, they immediately get Alana on a stretcher. I put her phone in her purse and hand it off to the paramedic that's asking Dallas to complete some kind of report.

"Shauntay, can you tell him exactly what happened?" Dallas asks.

Nodding, I do as told. The paramedic gives me a dumbfounded look when I share what caused the allergic reaction.

"You didn't remember that your best friend is allergic to pineapples?" he asks.

Dallas takes offense at the paramedic's tone. "My wife just came home from the hospital," he informs. "She's suffering from retrograde amnesia. There's a lot she doesn't remember, and if you don't believe her, I'll be more than happy to show you her discharge papers."

The paramedic looks from me to Dallas before getting in the ambulance and leaving.

"Do you want to follow them there?" Dallas asks.

"No. I think she'll be fine," I say, locking the door.

"You remember a lot about her, but you didn't remember that she's allergic to pineapple?"

I shrug. "I did get a weird feeling as I grabbed the tropical punch, but I wrote it off." Dallas nods before looking at me with widened eyes. I smile and ask, "You need anything?"

"I'm good," he says, walking down the hallway.

Taking a deep breath, I trail behind him. Though Alana is going to be fine, I don't know if Dallas and I are going to be. He still hasn't said anything about our marriage since the day I visited him at work. If what Alana said is true, and he does have a mistress, then I'd prefer him to be open about it instead of living a double life. It'll be much easier to end things with him now instead of when my memories return. What if prior me knew about the affair, and that's what made her want a divorce? Prior me was probably too embarrassed to tell Ashantee all the details, so that's why she shut down instead.

It's hard to believe that Dallas would even have an affair if he's been warding off Alana for twelve years. Prior me couldn't have known about Alana's feelings for Dallas because there's no way she would've remained friends with her. There's a lot to make sense of, but Dallas and I need to set things straight first. I've wasted the last month thinking he and I could find a new normal when the reality is that he may not even want to be with me.

"Have you thought about what I said when I visited you at work?" I ask, stopping him from ascending the stairs. "Did you make a decision about whether or not you want to rekindle our relationship?"

He stares at me, unsure how to respond.

"I won't accidentally give you tropical punch, so be honest with me."

"Your father taught me how to be a responsible man. He said that as the man of the house, it's my job to handle things and to honor my word. Because of that...because of our vows, the fact that we're married...and because I know there's a part of me that loves you, I do want to make our relationship work."

"Are you willing to start trying now?" I ask, approaching him. "With both of us having a clean slate and letting bygones be bygones?"

"I am."

"Then can we go on a date?"

He's taken aback. "What?"

"Let's go on a date," I repeat. "It can be something small, even if it's dinner and a movie."

He continues to stare at me in disbelief.

"Unless I've done something so terrible that our marriage can't be repaired."

Dallas stares at me for a while before saying, "Let's go on a date. I don't work weekends, so when I get in tomorrow, I'll take a nap and take you out."

I smile at him, unable to hide my excitement. "I have to go check my closet," I say, running up the steps. I stop halfway and face him. "Where are we going so I know how to dress? On second thought, don't tell me because I want to be surprised. I'll find something nice."

He chuckles. "You want me to plan it?"

"Duh!" I say, making it upstairs.

Perhaps thirty-year-old me wouldn't have let him off the hook so easily. Twenty-two-year-old me is just excited for another chance to get dolled up.

Chapter 8: Dallas Monroe

MARCH 16, 2022

Misty laughs at something on her phone as the movie we're supposed to be watching goes on commercial. She complained about me not seeing her in five days, so I decided to stop by before work. We're lying next to each other in bed, but I'm not touching her. I didn't even kiss her when I arrived. I can tell that she wants to have sex by the way she keeps pushing against me, but I'm not feeling it… at least not with her. I can't get Shauntay out of my mind. Seeing her take a shower and rubbing her down…

"Are you even paying attention to me?" Misty asks, sitting up. "You'll have to leave for work soon, but all you've done is watch TV."

"Chill, Misty. You wanted me to visit, so here I am."

"Whatever," she says, getting back on her phone.

My phone vibrates, and from the pattern I can tell it's Shauntay. Opening her message, I see a picture of her. She did her makeup, and her hair is in a ponytail. She's wearing a yellow with blue polka dots halter dress. I can't see her full body, but she's smiling while holding a pair of tongs. *Just finished cooking.*

You look cute, I reply back.

Thanks. I was hoping you'd like me in this outfit.

I think I like you in anything you put on, I reply, feeling myself blush. I'm just flirting with my wife, the woman I've been with since eighteen, yet I'm smiling like a kid at Chuck E. Cheese.

Why don't you come home so I can, Shauntay's incomplete message leaves me in excited anticipation.

Feed you? She suggests. Clearing my throat, I sit up.

Misty glances at me. "Who got you smiling like that?"

"I'm not smiling, but I'm finna head out."

Misty looks at me suspiciously before glancing at my pants. "You ain't never leave my place in that condition. Who were you texting?"

"I probably won't make it back before work. See you tomorrow... I think," I say before leaving.

***

Parking in the garage, I decide to leave my phone in my SUV. Misty's been blowing up my phone because of how I left her apartment, but she's no concern of mine right now.

"Hope I'm not too late for lunch," I tell Shauntay as I enter the kitchen.

She smiles at me while getting silverware out of the drawer. "You left your friend's house pretty quickly."

Shrugging, I wash my hands. "There wasn't anything good over there anyway."

"Why don't you sit on the back patio? I'm having lunch out there since it's warm today."

"You need any help?" I offer.

Shauntay shakes her head before we head to the patio, where I see lunch set up on the table.

"I made a fresh smoothie for us," she says as we walk to the table.

"What else did you make?" I ask, pulling out a chair for her.

She motions for me to sit instead, and as I do, she uncovers a plate of food. "Pan-seared salmon, green beans, and yellow rice. The rolls and cheesecake are store-bought because I didn't feel like baking much today."

I stare at her, incredulously.

"What's wrong? You allergic to seafood?" She frantically asks, covering the plate.

I slowly shake my head. "I'm not allergic to anything but pet hair."

"Then why are you staring at me like that?"

"Because this was the first meal you ever cooked for me."

Her face softens into a smile. "Really?"

"Your parents allowed me to spend spring break with y'all during sophomore year, and from what your Momma says, you got yourself worked up in a frenzy about cooking for me. She said you'd never made more than scrambled eggs in your life, but now that I was visiting, you were trying to be Lena Richard. She said you were watching videos and reading articles online, and when she tried to help, you told her no one else was cooking for your man but you."

Shauntay bursts out laughing, causing me to do the same. "What did everyone say about the food?" she asks when she catches her breath.

"They said it smelled delicious."

"What they say about how it tasted?"

"They said nothing because you only cooked enough for me," I say, smiling at her. "I thought it was delicious, just like I'm sure this is about to be."

"No need to keep you waiting any longer then," she says, uncovering the food and picking up a napkin. She tucks it into the top of my shirt before sitting on my lap.

I'm caught off guard, but I wrap my arms around her waist, showing that I don't want her to go anywhere. When Shauntay asked again about rekindling our relationship last week, I thought she just wanted to go on a date before calling it quits, but the complete opposite happened. I took her mini-golfing, and she had a ball. She kept touching me, and asking me for help. She made me feel wanted by her. A feeling I hadn't felt in a long time. The joy I felt when she smiled at me when she got a hole in one, and when she cheered me on as I played is a feeling I want to experience forever.

We make small talk as she feeds me, and even this small moment is intimate. While admiring how beautiful she looks in this dress, I catch her stealing a glimpse of me too. Her body language since she's been home has been telling me she wants to go further, and as much as I want to, I can't, because I know deep down there's a part of her that probably still wants a divorce.

"It's been a month since you've been home. Do you like it here? Do you think you made the right decision?" I ask.

She caresses my face while looking into my eyes. "I like it here with you," she answers. "Thanks for taking care of me, Dallas."

I feel all the walls that I've put up against her over the last two years tumbling down. I shouldn't be able to forgive her this quickly for shutting me out, cheating on me, and suggesting a divorce. There's no way I should let her back in so easily...right?

Shauntay moves closer as if she's going to kiss me, but I look away. "You mentioned cheesecake?"

She forces a smile as she stands up. "Yep. Let me get you a slice."

I can't punish her for her past decisions, nor do I want to, but now I feel like a deceiver. I should tell her how unhappy we were so that she isn't living in a fantasy... but I don't want to. I want to fall in love with her again.

An image of her and her coworker flashes in my mind, and my jaw tightens. Why should I be the one to live with the memories of our painful past while she gets to create new ones of bliss?

Chapter 9: Shauntay Dallas

MARCH 23, 2022

I drop the basket off at the exit of the grocery store before sprinting to my SUV. Dallas has been eating at home with me before going to work, which means I've been cooking earlier for him. Today, I'm making spaghetti, but I didn't realize we were out of pasta sauce. Though I know I have a few hours before it's time for him to leave, he'll be waking up soon, and I want the food to already be finished. Thankfully spaghetti doesn't take long, and I've already cooked the meat.

"Shauntay?!" someone calls as I'm unlocking the vehicle's door.

I don't want to turn in the direction it came from, but the voice sounds so familiar.

"Shauntay!" he calls again, and it sounds like a vehicle is slowing down.

Turning around, I see a man leaning out of his window.

"Yes?" I ask, opening my door and tossing the grocery bag inside.

"Where have you been? When you didn't reply to my messages, I feared the worst, but then Mr. Stanley said you're going to be on leave for a few months."

I give the man before me the most flummoxed look I can muster. Part of me just wants to get in the car, lock the door, and drive off. Another part of me feels at ease, however, as if I can trust this man.

"Do I know you?"

The man's mouth drops open as his eyes widen. "What do you mean, do you know me?" he asks, hurt in his tone. "We've been together for almost two years."

"Now I know you're lying. I'm a married woman," I say, getting in the car.

"Married?" the man scoffs. "You don't love Dallas."

I freeze; how does he know my husband's name?

"You don't want to be with him; that's why you started having an affair with me."

My eyes widen, and I hold my breath. Did I hear this man correctly? I hear a car door open and slam, and I grab my mace.

"Shauntay, it's me, Brian," the man says, slowly approaching me. "You've got to remember me. I was on the phone when you had the accident."

My mind is telling me that this man is crazy, but my body and emotions are saying he's telling the truth.

"What accident?" I ask, facing him.

"The one you had on Valentine's Day. You were on your way to see me," he says.

I gasp as a scene of me leaving a restaurant in a purple dress comes to mind. I'm telling Alana and some other women bye before getting into a dark blue car.

"You said a car was driving too close to you. I said to switch lanes, and you said you couldn't because—"

"I wasn't on the highway yet," I say, staring at Brian, still in disbelief.

"You remember," he says, smiling.

"The accident and phone call, yes. You, no. I have amnesia," I confess. "I haven't been able to remember much past college. I remember being on the phone, but not who I was talking to."

Brian's lip trembles as he registers my words. He reaches into his pocket, and I push the lid up on my mace and aim it at him.

"It's just my phone," he says, showing it to me. "Look."

He shows me a picture of us at a restaurant. It's someone's birthday since there's a cake on the table. He shows me another picture of us kissing. Then he shows one where I'm in lingerie sitting on his lap. I don't recognize the bedroom we're in, but I'm kissing his neck while posing for the camera.

"You've gotta remember us," he says, heartbroken. "We love each other. You and Dallas met with a divorce lawyer."

A sharp twinge stabs the side of my head, and as I close my eyes, I see an image of a business card with the name Justin Campbell on top. I stare at Brian when I open my eyes. Something deep down is whispering that he's telling the truth, but it doesn't make sense. Why would I leave Dallas for this man? He's not even my type.

"Brian, I understand that you're hurt, but I'm not the woman in those pictures anymore. I am not leaving my husband, nor do I want to continue having an affair with you."

His eyes swell with tears, and I stare at him, wondering if past me felt as strongly about him as he does for her. "Remember your tattoo? You got a butterfly to symbolize that you broke out of your cocoon and you're ready to fly away."

Now it makes sense why Dallas was so upset about seeing the tattoo. "I'm not flying away," I sternly tell Brian. "I'm not sure why you and past me started having an affair, but it ended the day the accident happened. Have a nice day," I say, closing the door and starting the engine.

As I drive off, I take one last look at the heartbroken man in the parking lot. I consider asking him not to reach out to Dallas concerning our affair, but if Brian hasn't reached out before, he probably won't now. The stabbing pain returns, causing me to wince as I turn out of the parking lot to head home. The more I try to remember my life with Brian, the more my head hurts. It's as if my mind does not want me to remember my affair. I didn't get a headache when I remembered my father's funeral and the death of my son, so why is Brian causing so much pain?

"Hey, Peaches," Dallas says when I enter the kitchen. "I was about to call you."

"I had to run to the store," I answer. "I didn't know we were out of pasta sauce."

"You don't look so well," he says, taking the grocery bag from me.

"I ran into someone... I used to know."

"Who was it?"

I hesitate between telling the honest truth and a fabricated version. "Someone from work," I say, watching for his reaction.

He raises an eyebrow. "Did you remember them?"

"Nope," I say, washing my hands to start boiling the noodles. "I told them to leave me alone too."

I glance at Dallas and see him with a clenched jaw. I offer him a smile.

"I'll be finished cooking in no time. Why don't you watch some TV until the food is ready?"

He nods before walking to the living room. After putting water in the pot to boil, I take my phone out and scroll through my messages, looking for Brian's name. I don't find it, but I see a message thread with an unknown number. After clicking on it, I realize that it's my conversation with Brian. I skim through some messages before becoming completely disgusted. I delete the thread, and for once, I hope my memories, at least of him, never return.

Chapter 10: Dallas Monroe

MARCH 26, 2022

Taking a deep breath, I knock on Misty's door. I hear her look through the peephole before unlocking the door.

"It's five-thirty in the morning, Dallas!" Misty scolds. "Why didn't you use your key instead of waking me up?"

"Because we need to talk," I say as she moves out of the way so I can enter the apartment.

"We can talk later. Go take a shower, and when I wake up, I'll tell you what I want you to buy to make it up to me."

"I didn't come here to take a shower, Misty."

She faces me with an eyebrow raised. "You just got off of work, and you're sweaty. You ain't finna get in my bed smelling and looking like that."

"I came to apologize and return your key."

Misty looks at me suspiciously. "You can keep the key, and if you're talking about apologizing for ignoring me for the last week, then you can make it up to me by buying everything in my online cart."

"That's not what—"

"I don't know what's been up with you lately. You ran out of my apartment the other day, clearly hard, ignored my calls and texts, and then just showed up here like everything's fine? Where the hell have you been, Dallas? What female are you running behind now?"

"Shauntay and I—"

"It's always you and that damned woman. When you're pissed, it's Shauntay this. When you're happy, it's Shauntay that. I don't want to hear her name in my home again. I don't care what y'all have going on. Unless you're telling me that the divorce is finalized, I don't want you to ever mention her name in my presence!"

I place Misty's apartment key on the counter before looking into her eyes. "My wife and I have decided to work things out. I thought doing it over the phone would be heartless, so I came in person to tell you that things between us are over."

Misty's face drops. "What do you mean it's over, Dallas?" she whispers.

"I'm going to stay with my wife. I don't want to keep seeing you on the side and give you false hope for a divorce that's never going to happen."

Misty's eyes swell with tears. "So, the last year and a half didn't mean shit? Everything we did, all those times I was there for you, every time you said you loved me—they were all lies?!"

"Of course not, Misty. They meant a lot to me. Thank you for being there for me, and while I do love you, I can never love you the way I love Shauntay."

Misty grimaces at the mention of my wife's name, but I don't care. "Shauntay has been my best friend since we were eighteen, and we've experienced almost everything together. I'm not going to throw that away."

"What about her cheating on you?"

I exhale heavily. "I'm still working through that, but I've forgiven her. She obviously doesn't even remember having an affair. She and I were given a second chance for our marriage, and I'm not going to waste that opportunity. I apologize for any pain I'm causing you, but I'm going to remain married."

I turn to leave as I see the tears fall from her eyes. I knew this was going to be hard, but it had to be done eventually.

"You can't just leave me like this," Misty calls before I can exit. "Don't I get a say? Don't I get the chance to fight for us?"

"There is no us, Misty," I say, facing her.

"There is an us; there has been an us for almost two years. You think I'm going to let that go so easily?!" She yells, pushing me. "I'm going to tell everyone about us," she says, tearfully. "I'm going to post it online, and I'm going to tell Shauntay."

Closing my eyes, I take a deep breath. I'd contemplated how things would go if Misty retaliated. "If that's what you want to do, then fine," I say, opening my eyes. "I was going to come clean about the affair anyway, but if you want to be the one to tell a woman who has nothing to lose that you've been sleeping with her husband for the past two years, then may the odds ever be in your favor," I say before turning to the door. "I'm not the only one with a mean streak, and Shauntay has been detained for assaulting someone before," I say, chuckling. "I don't care what you do with my stuff. Throw it away, burn it—whatever. Goodbye, Misty," I say, leaving the apartment and closing the door behind me.

I speed home and pray I don't get a ticket. Though Shauntay is usually asleep when I get off of work, unless I ask her to have breakfast waiting for me, she usually wakes up to greet me when I get home. I don't want her to think I'm doing something I shouldn't be.

I peep into the master bedroom when I get in.

"Hey, Dallas," Shauntay says.

"Hey," I say, walking to the bed. "I'm surprised you're still up."

"I had a nightmare," she says, putting her phone on the nightstand. "I've been watching videos on social media since that's what people do nowadays," she says, causing me to chuckle. "You're home kinda late."

"I had to take care of something. I'm sorry if I worried you." Shauntay looks into my eyes, and I take her hand in mine. "I won't be late again unless it's work or traffic related," I promise.

"Are you going to shower?"

"I'm heading there now."

"Can you shower in here?" she asks, and I look at her, puzzled. "Afterward, can you...sleep in here with me, please?" I hold my breath, as I stare at her; there's no way I heard her correctly. "I don't want to be alone."

"Okay," I say, letting her hand go.

My mind swirls with thoughts as I enter the en suite bathroom. I'm confused and apprehensive at the same time. While turning on the shower, I go to the walk-in closet and grab a towel and washcloth. The second to last time I was in here, it was to clean out my side of the closet. I came in here once after that, and I saw that Shauntay had moved her clothes to where mine used to be. Now, my side is empty again. She also bought a small dresser to keep our towels in.

I grab what I need, shower, and reenter the bedroom in my boxers. Shauntay is back on her phone.

She sits up when she sees me. "Which side is yours?"

I nod to the left side, and she moves over. I'm still feeling a series of emotions. Never in a million years did I think I'd ever be back in this bed, and certainly not beside her. I slowly get in bed, rest my phone on the dresser, and look at Shauntay to see what's next.

She turns her back to me and scoots back. Hesitantly, I put an arm around her waist. "Tell me about your nightmare," I whisper.

Shauntay makes herself comfortable under my arm as she begins telling me about her whodunnit adventure with Jessica Fletcher. I can't help but laugh while listening to how she got separated from Jessica and the murderer chased her through a toy store.

"It's not funny," Shauntay complains, hitting my hand.

"That may be scary," I say, catching my breath. "But I told you to stop binging those murder shows all day long."

"Whatever," she mumbles. "I just want to go back to sleep."

"Go back to sleep," I say, chuckling. "I'll take the first watch against the deranged killer."

"You'll keep me safe?" Shauntay whispers.

Nothing's amusing anymore now that my wife has asked me to protect her. "I won't let anything happen to you, Peaches," I assure her, tightening my grip around her.

Her face is still turned away from me, so I don't know what she's expressing, but she places her hand on mine.

***

"Hey, sleepyhead," Shauntay greets when I enter the living room.

"Hey," I say, glancing at the TV. She's binging *Murder, She Wrote,* again.

"You haven't learned your lesson," I tease.

She tosses a throw pillow at my face. "I had to do something while you were sleeping. It's one in the afternoon."

"Try a safer show, like Scooby-Doo.

"I'm actually bored. Momma teaches classes at the senior center, Ashantee works, and I call your mom so much, I'm starting to think I may not be her favorite daughter-in-law anymore."

"But I'm an only child."

"Exactly," she says before I laugh.

Of course, Shauntay's bored. Just a few days ago, she reorganized the pantry and every closet in the house. She's alone for hours at a time when she normally would've been at work. "How about we go out today? Is there anything you want to do?"

Shauntay pauses her show as she thinks. "I want to do something active and fun, like mini golf."

Stroking my beard, I say, "How about we go to the gun range?"

Shauntay's eyes widen. "The gun range?" she asks, shocked by the suggestion.

"Yes. That way you can protect yourself and Jessica Fletcher the next time y'all go to a toy store."

Shauntay rolls her eyes. "Are we even licensed owners?"

"Since we've been married," I say, lifting my shirt to show her my gun.

She smiles. "That's sexy."

"The gun?" I ask, confused.

"The abs," she answers, causing me to blush. I didn't develop muscles until I took the warehouse job. "Do I have a gun?" she asks.

"Yes. It was recovered from the accident, and I put it in our safe."

"What kind of gun is it?"

"A small handgun; it can fit in most of your purses."

"Let's go," she says, standing up. "But I don't think I remember how to shoot."

"I'll give you a couple of pointers. Look in your wallet and see if your membership card is in there."

"Membership?" she asks, grabbing her purse from the hall closet.

"Yeah, we're members of Ponder Gun Range."

"Ooh, that sounds fancy," she says as we head to the garage.

"Yep. It's a prominent Black-owned, indoor and outdoor gun range."

***

"This is your gun," I say, placing it on the counter. I walk her through putting the safety on and off before showing her how to insert bullets. "Now you need to choose a point, aim, and fire."

Nodding, Shauntay walks to a target, lifts her gun, and fires. She barely hits a shoulder, and she stumbles a little from the kickback.

"What was that?" I ask, laughing. "Did you even aim?"

"I did, but I closed my eyes."

"Try again," I say, walking toward her. "You have very good aim."

"I do?" she asks, surprised.

"You used to," I say, chuckling. I instruct her to face the target again and coach her through aiming. "You got this," I say, putting a hand over her shaking hands and an arm around her waist. "Relax," I whisper into her ear. "You ready?"

"Mhmm," Shauntay answers before aiming, firing, and hitting the target right in the center.

"There you go."

"I did it," she cheers before facing me. "We did it," she says, looking into my eyes and placing the gun on the counter.

My heartbeat increases as she caresses my cheek and brings my face toward hers. Just like the first time we kissed in college, I freeze, too nervous to make the first move. Shauntay kisses me. It's just a peck, but it's the first time we've done anything like this since she's been home. She pulls away and looks into my eyes when I don't kiss her back.

"It's been years since I've fired my rifle," I say, letting her go and opening my rifle case.

Shauntay sighs. "You know how to shoot a rifle?"

"Pretty well."

"What have you been shooting?"

"Your dad and I used to go hunting all the time.

"No way."

"Yes, way," I say, chuckling. "He's the one who taught me about shooting, and we went on our first hunting trip shortly after."

"Hunting?" she incredulously asks again.

"Just watch," I say before loading the rifle and getting a fresh target paper.

I effortlessly hit every point on the paper, and Shauntay claps. "You really are good," she compliments. "So, what did you and Daddy used to do on these trips? Shoot cans and stuff?"

"Cans?" I scoff. "No. We hunted deer, wild pigs, turkeys—"

"That's so cruel!" Shauntay says, covering her eyes. "What did y'all do with it?"

Chuckling, I put the gun down. "We took it to the processor, brought it home, and your mom would cook it."

"My mom would cook *what*?" Shauntay asks, alarmed.

"Whatever we brought home."

"My mother would never!"

"You used to cook it too," I say, laughing.

"Me?" she doubtfully asks.

"You always used to say, 'If my man is out there hunting, then I'm finna be at home with the stove on.'"

"That doesn't even sound like me!" She objects.

"Your mom's house is down the street, you wanna go ask her?"

"Yep," she says, folding her arms.

Nodding, we empty our guns before packing up and leaving.

***

"What brings y'all by?" Ms. Lisa asks when we enter the living room. She and Ashantee are sitting on the couch, watching TV.

"Hey, Tee," Shauntay says, hugging her sister before sitting beside her.

"Momma, can you tell your child that me, and Pops used to go hunting?" I ask, plopping in the armchair.

"All the time," Ms. Lisa agrees. "They used to go away on weekend trips and all."

"Now can you tell your child who used to cook the game we brought back?"

"Me and you, of course," Ms. Lisa says, looking at Shauntay.

"Momma, ain't no way you used to let me cook deer and all that."

"You were the best one in the family who prepared it," Ashantee says.

Shauntay's jaw drops, causing Ms. Lisa, to chuckle. "Yep. Your favorite line was—"

"If my man is out there hunting, then I'm finna be in the kitchen with the stove on," Ms. Lisa and Ashantee say at the same time.

Standing up, Shauntay shakes her head and waves her hands back and forth. "This is too much. I'm going to look around my room."

I chuckle as she leaves.

"How are things going between you two?" Ms. Lisa asks once Shauntay is up the steps.

"I don't have any complaints," I say, shrugging.

"How's the marriage?" she asks, catching me off guard. I silently stare at her, and she chuckles. "You think I didn't know y'all were going through a rough patch?"

I glance at Ashantee, who shakes her head.

"No one had to tell me anything. I saw the way you watched her go up the stairs just now. I haven't seen you look at her like that in years...not since she was pregnant."

Sighing, I lean back in the chair. "We were trying to keep it from you. Shauntay said it would break your heart if you found out the truth, so we put on a façade."

Ms. Lisa rolls her eyes. "Y'all should've been asking for help instead of pretending like everything was okay."

"Pops had just died, and she said she didn't want to put any more stress on you."

"Even if y'all didn't want to come to me, y'all could've gone to Ashantee, the pastor, or even marriage counseling. Pretending that everything was alright does more damage than harm."

"If only you knew," I mumble.

"What's the plan for you two now?" Ashantee asks.

"Things have been great between us lately. We've been spending time together and going on dates," I say, smiling. "I feel like I'm getting to know her all over again...the *her* I fell in love with."

"And what about the other thing?" Ashantee pries.

I glance at Ms. Lisa before returning to Ashantee. "The other thing is squashed." Which is true. I blocked Misty's number, and I haven't seen anything online. "Shauntay's birthday is coming up," I say, looking at Ashantee and Ms. Lisa. "I'd like to do something special. Take her somewhere special for the weekend or something."

"Take her to the cabins in North Georgia," Ashantee suggests.

"The cabins?" Ms. Lisa criticizes.

"Yes, Momma. It's a lot more romantic than it sounds," Ashantee says, rubbing her stomach. "How do you think I ended up in this predicament?"

We all laugh before I say, "Please send me the details. I'd like for us to stay for about three or four days."

"What are y'all going to be doing for three or four days?" Ms. Lisa asks, raising an eyebrow.

"C'mon, Momma," I say, pulling out my phone to distract myself.

Shauntay descends the stairs then. "I don't remember this," she says, displaying a picture frame.

"I don't remember that either," Ms. Lisa says, glaring at me.

I laugh after inspecting the picture. Shauntay is dressed as Wonder Woman with an extra short skirt. I'm dressed as Batman with my arms around her waist and kissing her cheek.

"I haven't seen that picture since the day we took it. We went to a costume party," I explain. "You got an extra short skirt to show off your new tattoo."

"A tattoo I didn't know she had until I was helping her get ready for her wedding," Ms. Lisa scolds. "Your father and I did not approve of you going to Halloween parties."

"It was a costume party," I clarify.

"On Halloween?" Ms. Lisa asks.

I nod, still amused. "You had to come home for the weekend because it was your aunt's birthday or something," I tell Shauntay as she sits beside me. "Your family had a dinner party for her here, but you 'got sick,'" I chuckle, using air quotes. "You got dressed and snuck out of the house. I was waiting outside, and we went to the party together."

"I can't believe it," Ms. Lisa says, shaking her head. "Your father swore up and down that you wouldn't be problematic."

"It's okay, Momma. Dads are allowed to get things wrong sometimes," Ashantee chimes in.

"You knew about it and covered for her," I say, throwing Ashantee under the bus as well.

"You weren't supposed to know that! Tay tells you too much," Ashantee whines.

"Y'all take that picture and get out of my house. I don't want anything concerning Halloween anywhere near me," Ms. Lisa says.

Laughing, I stand up and extend my hand to Shauntay. "No need for us to overstay our welcome."

Shauntay playfully sticks her tongue out at her mother and sister before walking with me out of the house. We get to my SUV, but I don't unlock the door.

"What's wrong?"

"Can I get a do-over?"

Shauntay looks at me, confused. "A do-over for what?"

"You kissed me earlier, and I didn't return the gesture."

"Oh, that," Shauntay, says, looking away. "Don't worry about it. Obviously, you're not ready to go there with me."

I wrap an arm around her waist and bring her to me. "I am ready, Shauntay," I say, looking into her eyes and caressing her cheek. I bring her face to mine and kiss her. I even caress and squeeze her butt. She wraps her arms around my neck and pulls me closer.

"Momma, they're making out in front of your house!" Ashantee yells.

Shauntay glares at her sister. "Tattletale," she says before returning her attention to me. "Why are you staring at me like that?"

I continue caressing her cheek while staring into her eyes. I'm overwhelmed with too much emotion to answer her question. "We're going away for your birthday next month, so don't make any plans."

Smiling, Shauntay kisses me again.

Chapter 11: Shauntay Monroe

APRIL 9, 2022

"Girl, you're going on and on like you even remember how to put on lingerie," Ashantee laughs as I walk her to the front door at my house.

"Sis, putting on lingerie isn't the goal; it's getting him to take it off," I say before we laugh again.

We'd just gotten in from a day of pampering and shopping, and Ashantee needed to use the bathroom before leaving. I bought an assortment of lingerie in various colors because I am determined to enjoy my right to my husband's body.

"When are y'all leaving?" Tee asks as I open the door.

"After he wakes up and finishes packing. That should give me enough time to wash these," I say, lifting the bag with lingerie.

"You're going to come back pregnant," Tee laughs as she heads to her car.

"If not, I'm going to have fun trying."

Tee shakes her head. "Enjoy the rest of your birthday, girl," she says before I lock the door.

I head down the hall, but before I can ascend the steps to the laundry room, the doorbell rings. I hesitate about opening it before going to see who it is. Dallas is right upstairs if I need him, and I've since started carrying my gun again.

Looking through the sidelight, I see a light-skinned woman around my age. Though her face is cold and hard, her eyes look nervous.

"May I help you?" I ask, opening the door.

She stands straight while looking me directly in the eyes. "Are you Shauntay?"

Her tone is sharp, causing me to realize she's not as nervous as she looks. "I am. Who are you?"

"I'm Misty, the one Dallas has been with for the last year and a half," she proudly announces. "I've got videos, pictures, and messages. He stopped loving you when he started loving me. He's been coming over to my house before work, and he's been grabbing more than just a bite to eat."

I rub my hand down my face. When I open my eyes, I see Misty smirking. After taking a deep breath, I ask, "Are you finished?"

Misty's expression changes from prideful to astonished. "Am I finished? Did you hear what I said?"

"Yes," I say, opening the front door wider. "You bravely and boldly came to my house to tell me about an affair my husband is clearly no longer having. What are you expecting to accomplish?"

"Aren't you upset or heartbroken?"

"About my husband dumping you? No. I'm quite thrilled actually," I say, stepping closer. "Why exactly did you come here to tell me this news in person? Surely you could've found me online. You also could've left a letter in the mailbox or something. Why did you feel the need to tell me face-to-face?"

Misty stumbles to find the right words.

"Do you want to fight?" I ask, raising my hands, causing my shirt to rise also. Misty's eyes widen as she stares at my gun. "Don't worry, that's just for strangers. Since you and I have so much in common, I'll use my fists."

"Why aren't you upset?"

"You think I'm not upset that my marriage was bad enough to make my husband step out a year and a half ago? You think I'm not upset that he had to run to another woman to get everything he should've been getting from me? I can't rewrite the past, but the fact that you're here proves that he chose me over you. You can't expect to play house with someone's husband and not get hurt."

"Y'all were supposed to get a divorce," she trembles, tears falling from her eyes.

Looking at her reminds me of my encounter with Brian. How in the world did Dallas and I manage to build such strong bonds with other people within two years?

"We are not getting a divorce," I confidently say, looking into her eyes. "So, I suggest you leave my husband alone and drive away in your car before you get carried away in an ambulance. I don't play about my husband nor protecting our marriage."

Misty tearfully walks to the driveway, gets in her car, and leaves. After locking the door, I return to my shopping bags that are by the staircase. There's a part of me that's demanding I become irate, but I silence her. We were both having an affair, and though it hurts, I told Dallas that I want to leave the past in the past and start anew. Therefore, I won't let what happened just now ruin my birthday or the four-day trip he planned for us.

I toss the lingerie into the washing machine for a quick cycle before entering the bedroom.

"Hey, Peaches," Dallas says, waking up.

"Hey," I say, smiling at him.

"You ready to go?"

"I'm doing a quick load of laundry, and I want to shower before we leave. I need about an hour."

"Two hours, got it," he teases.

"You aren't even packed yet."

"Nope, but I'll be finished before you even step foot in the shower. Judging by the time and traffic, we'll make it to the cabins in time for dinner. I made reservations at a top-notch restaurant for your birthday."

"Then I better pick out something sexy," I tease.

"Any dress you wear is sexy."

"Then I guess I'll wear a dress," I say, winking before entering the bathroom.

I'm not sure if Dallas knows about the affair I had or not. All I know is that he took care of me at a time he didn't have to. Because of that, I won't be petty or bitter. Somehow, we were given a second chance to make this marriage work, and I'm not going to blow it.

Chapter 12: Dallas Monroe

APRIL 9, 2022

"Here we are," I tell Shauntay as I pull into the cabin resort Ashantee told me about.

Shauntay pauses the R&B playlist she made for our trip before letting go of my hand. "This looks promising."

"We're a few minutes late for our dinner reservation, so let's go to the restaurant before our cabin."

"Okay," Shauntay says, taking off her seatbelt. "I already checked us in online anyway."

Nodding, I pull into a parking spot and make my way to her door. We enter the restaurant hand in hand, and as we're waiting for the waiter to show us to our table, Shauntay unbuttons her trench coat. I help her out of it, and I'm immediately captivated. She's wearing a low-cut, sleeveless, black and nude lace dress that stops just above her knees. Her braids are in a high ponytail, showing off the silver jewelry set I got her for our fifth anniversary. She finishes her look with black heels and red lipstick. She faces me, and I know there's such a thing as love at first sight. She has me captivated, just like she did the first day we met.

"You think this dress is too tight?" she whispers to me before swiping a hand across her stomach.

Shauntay never returned to her former size after the pregnancy, and I never pressured her to. I still love everything about her body; from the scar she developed after the C-section to her cute and chubby waist.

"You're breathtaking," I finally reply.

Shauntay smiles before taking my hand in hers again as we follow the waiter to our table. While walking, I can't help but notice men checking her out. I want to tell her to put her jacket back on while scowling at the men for looking at my wife, but then I remember that Shauntay and I aren't wearing rings. I stopped wearing mine when she demanded that I sleep in the guest room; I'm not sure when she stopped wearing hers. To onlookers, she's my date, not my wife.

The restaurant is dimly lit. The black and white décor makes it look elegant. There are black iron cushioned chairs and tables with white tablecloths draped on top. Flower vases serve as centerpieces at the round tables.

The waiter tries to pull out Shauntay's chair when we get to the table, but I place my hand on the chair. "I got it," I tell him.

Shauntay chuckles as she sits down. We order quickly and enjoy small talk throughout the meal. Though I'm having a great time, guilt weighs heavily on my chest.

"I have to be honest with you, Peaches," I say as she's perusing the dessert menu.

She places the menu down to give me her full attention. "Okay."

I struggle to find the right words. Deciding to speak from the heart, I move my chair closer to hers. "I don't know the consequences of me admitting this, but I can't carry it around anymore. Shauntay, our marriage was at rock bottom before your accident. We secretly met with a divorce lawyer three weeks before the accident. We agreed to continue living in the house together, but you were doing your own thing, and I was doing mine. We put on a façade at church and in front of our friends and family. I'd been sleeping in the guest room way before your accident. About seven months after our son died, I started having an affair," I say, watching for her reaction. Shauntay silently listens with her best poker face. "I'd be lying if I said I didn't care for her, but I've since cut ties with her. I don't want to invite you into a lie, so I'm laying all the cards on the table."

"Thanks for telling me," she says, reaching for my hand. I move my hand away, though.

"You may not remember this, but you were having an affair too," I share. Her eyes widen before she returns to her poker face. "I saw the messages, and I was tempted to confront him, as well as to tell you that I no longer want to be with you. Unsure of what to do, I decided to wait it out and see if you'd regain your memory. The more I waited, the more I fell in love with you again," I say before taking a deep breath. "Peaches, you're caring and kind. You're beautiful inside and out, and I realized that I don't want to make it work with anyone but you. You're my best friend and lover. I want to keep experiencing life with you, but I don't want to do it under a false pretense. I want us to both know the truth and decide how we're going to move forward."

Shauntay reaches for my hand again, and I let her take it. "Thank you for telling me that," she says.

I examine her eyes to see if she's upset or disappointed, but I don't see either emotion. Part of me expected her to become dramatic or loud, but she's calm, and her eyes are welcoming.

"I've heard, and I've had inklings, that our marriage wasn't in the best shape, but hearing you come clean about it means a lot. It shows me that you won't hide any secrets from me. I found out about your affair a while ago."

"I'm sorry."

Shauntay chuckles. "You don't have to keep apologizing for that. After meeting Misty, I have an idea as to why you fell for her." I stare at Shauntay with widened eyes, but she pats my hand. "Misty came by the house earlier, but I don't think she'll be a problem anymore."

I want to ask for more details, but I infer that the less I know about their encounter, the better.

"I didn't know about my affair until I ran into Brian at the grocery store. I don't think he'll be an issue either, but I'm sorry too, Dallas," she says, looking into my eyes. "I am revolted by my affair, and you have my word that I'll never do that again. There may have been a time when he meant something to me, but I couldn't care less about him now. We've clearly made awful decisions over the last two years, but the fact that we're here tonight proves that we are renewing our commitment to one another. While we may not be able to have our marriage return to what it used to be, we can continue moving forward in this new season."

"Is that what you really want to do?" I whisper.

"Yes, if you want to."

"I would love that. Shauntay, I love you, and I will never love anyone else the way I love you."

"Good," she says, smiling. "I love you, too. Now let's have some dessert." She reaches for the menu but looks at me instead. "Unless you're trying to have some dessert when we get to the room," she says, licking her lips. I chuckle to hide my blushing. "You've gotta tell me: have I always been this horny? Because I've been very horny these last couple of weeks."

"You've always had a high sex drive," I say, facing her again. "But I've never had any issues satisfying it."

Shauntay bites her lip before the waiter returns to our table. "Can I get you anything else?" he asks.

"We need the check. Pronto," Shauntay says, still staring at me.

Clearing my throat, I stand up and extend a hand to her. "Charge it to room 29," I tell the waiter before escorting Shauntay to the exit.

Once we're in the car, we drive around the resort until we find our cabin. After parking, we take our luggage inside, unlocking the cabin door with the code emailed to us. The room is very romantic. There are rose petals around the bed, champagne chilling on the nightstand, and a covered assortment of chocolates and fruits on the table. There's a jetted jacuzzi with rose petals around it too. The bathroom is a bit on the small side, but that's because of the large shower with a glass wall that gives the person on the bed a full view of the person showering.

"I like this," Shauntay says, walking into the bathroom.

"Where are you going?" I ask, locking the door behind us.

"I need to change."

"Change?" I scoff. "Why don't you strip instead?"

She chuckles as she faces me. "And let all the cute lingerie I bought go to waste?"

"No," I say, taking her hand in mine and leading her to the bed. "We have three more nights here; you'll have plenty of time to show me what you bought. Right now, you owe me some dessert."

Shauntay pushes me on the bed while standing in front of me. "I might've thrown on a little something under here in case something like this were to happen," she says, taking her dress off.

She's wearing a matching navy, lace bra and panty set. She sits on top of me and unbuttons my dress shirt as we kiss. She admires my shirtless body before unfastening my pants. I'm turned on by her eagerness, but I enjoy being dominant. Once my pants are off, I roll over so that she's under me. I kiss her neck while taking off her bra. I kiss all over her body as I work my way to her waist. I use my teeth to pull her panty down, and as I work my way back up, I kiss and bite her peach tattoo, the tattoo she got because of me.

I satisfy my sweet tooth before easing inside of her. Being inside of Shauntay feels like being home. There's no need for condoms like there was with Misty. I love how she feels, and I can't believe I let this go. I can't believe I gave someone else the chance to satisfy me. I should've fought harder for us two years ago. I stare at Shauntay, who's moaning with every stroke. Ain't no way she let another man enjoy her like this. Ain't no way—

"Hey," Shauntay says, cupping my face. "Stay out of your head. I need you to focus on what's going on here." She kisses my face while wrapping her arms around my neck. She beckons me to roll over so she can get on top. "I don't need you to get soft on me now," she says, running her hands down my chest. "I'm just getting started."

"Go crazy then, baby," I say, wrapping my arms around her waist.

***

I rub Shauntay's back as she snores on my chest. As I replay the night's events, I think about the men checking out Shauntay at the restaurant, and the fact that she doesn't have a ring. Our anniversary is in a few months, and a new wedding set would be a great idea. Shauntay doesn't remember her first wedding set...or our wedding...or our engagement. Perhaps instead of trying to have her remember old memories, I should be helping her create new ones.

I kiss her forehead and caress her butt.

"You better relax before you start something again," she mumbles. I kiss her cheek, and she puts her hands in my boxers.

Chapter 13: Shauntay Monroe

MAY 30, 2022

I fasten my necklace as Dallas enters our bathroom. "Can I come downstairs now?" I ask, glaring at him.

He chuckles. "Yes, Peaches. You can come down, but let me get a look at you."

Sighing, I get off of the bathroom vanity's stool and face him. I'm wearing a long, strapless, green dress with open-toed wedges. I decided to style my hair in a twist-out despite knowing that it rains in Metro-Atlanta every Memorial Day weekend.

"You look beautiful," Dallas says as I spin around. "Your back is a little ashy though," he says, chuckling.

"Probably because it's still healing," I say, handing him the moisturizer.

During my birthday trip, I decided I wanted to get a new tattoo to cover up the butterfly one on my back. I didn't care what I got as long as it was pretty and large enough to cover up the butterfly. Dallas agreed to get one with me, and we decided to get matching tattoos again. We both got two interlocked crowns. One has his name, and the other has mine. He got his on his back too.

"I don't understand why I couldn't help with the cookout. I could've made something or helped decorate," I say as he anoints my back.

"Our friends and family volunteered to do all of that. Everyone agreed that you should relax."

"Everyone but me," I whine. "You know I've been enjoying cooking. I've even gained some followers from posting my videos online," I proudly say.

"Well, now you can enjoy the cookout," Dallas says, placing the moisturizer bottle on the counter. "C'mon. Everyone can't wait to see you."

I roll my eyes as I follow him out of our room. Our close family and friends were invited to our house, courtesy of Dallas. I initially wanted to go to the beach this weekend, but he insisted on us having a gathering at our house.

Coming down the steps and entering the kitchen, I hear music coming from the backyard. I smile, excited to start socializing and dancing.

"Hey, everyone!" I say when Dallas opens the backdoor for me.

I'm greeted by a series of salutations. I see people I remember and people whose faces I only remember from the albums in the house. Dallas and I walk under a green and purple balloon arch. I want to ask why there's a balloon arch at a cookout, and I freeze, wondering if today is Dallas' birthday also. I know he told me when it was when I came home from the hospital, but I don't remember it now.

"Shauntay," Dallas says, standing in front of me, "we've been through a lot these last couple of months. I almost lost you, in more ways than one. During this time, we've opened up to each other about a lot. We even had the chance to experience things for the first time again."

"You mean like the tattoos or...dessert in the cabin?" I ask before winking at him.

He chuckles. "Our recent time together makes me feel like I've fallen in love with you again."

"That's sweet because I feel like I've fallen in love with you for the first time," I say, causing our guests to laugh.

"I know there's a lot you don't remember, and I've accepted that there's nothing I can do to bring them back. Therefore, I've decided that we should make new memories together, like this one," he says, reaching into his pocket.

I raise an eyebrow as I look at him skeptically. He gets on one knee, and I gasp as I cover my mouth with both hands.

"Shauntay Renae Sanford, will you marry me?"

"What?" I incredulously ask before inspecting our guests' faces.

Momma, Ashantee, and Ms. Sandra are smiling at me. Our guests have their phones out, recording, I assume.

"My knees aren't as young as they used to be, Peaches, and this concrete slab isn't comfortable," Dallas says before everyone laughs. "So, what do you say? Think you can meet me at the altar one more time?" he asks, opening the ring box.

"Yes!" I say, jumping onto him. He catches me and lifts me up. "You really want to marry me again?"

"Of course. Why should I be the only one to remember the most wonderful day of our lives?" he asks, slipping the ring on my finger.

"You're so sweet," I say before kissing him.

When Dallas lets me go, Manny, Ashantee's husband, turns on an LED sign that reads 'She Said 'Yes,' and places it under the arch. Dallas and I pose in front of it as our loved ones take pictures of us.

"Isn't our anniversary in June?" I ask Dallas when the congratulations have concluded. He nods. "Can we have our ceremony on the same day? Let's make it small and intimate, but I want to do the whole ordeal. I want a dress, a bouquet, bridesmaids...and I want you in a suit," I say, biting my lip.

Dallas smiles. "If that's what you want, Peaches. Our anniversary is on a weekday, but let's see if the church can accommodate, and let's make it happen," he says before kissing me again.

Chapter 14: Shauntay Monroe

June 28, 2022

"I have a new tattoo, Momma," I joke when we're finished taking pictures. Momma rolls her eyes as Ashantee laughs. "I didn't want the tradition of her finding out about my tattoos on my wedding day to die."

"I'm surprised you got a man's name tatted on you," Ashantee states.

I shrug. "No big deal," I reply as we hear a knock on the chamber door.

"It's time," Ms. Sandra says before walking out.

Ashantee hugs me before exiting with our two cousins.

"How are you feeling?" Momma asks when we're alone.

"I'm fine," I say, staring at myself in the mirror. "This dress shows my curves off better than the first one," I say before looking at my butt. My wedding gown is strapless with a sweetheart cut and jewels throughout. My hair is in a bun with curly bangs, despite Momma telling me to wear my hair down to hide my tattoo.

"Be serious, child," she demands.

"I'm a bit nervous, but I shouldn't be. Legally, Dallas and I are already married. To him this is a vow renewal...and though I guess it should be that to me too, this feels like my first time getting married. I wish Daddy were here," I say before sighing. "But he's in my heart, and that'll have to be enough."

Momma hands me my bouquet before we exit the chamber. "You know how we sin and ask God for forgiveness, and He forgives and loves us as if we never messed up?"

I glance at her before looking forward as we enter the foyer. What does this have to do with Daddy's absence? "Yeah, I know that, Momma."

"Marriage is like that too sometimes. I don't condone abusive or toxic relationships, but healthy marriages go through their share of valleys. The only way to successfully move forward is to forgive and love as if no one ever messed up."

I think about her words as we wait for the sanctuary doors to open. I haven't held any grudges against Dallas. Alana, on the other hand, I told to never contact me or my husband again. She's forgiven, though. I haven't heard from Brian since our run-in, and Dallas hasn't heard from Misty, as far as I know. We're good on the forgiveness part.

The music for my entry begins, and Momma and I lock arms as the doors open. I hear gasps and receive looks of admiration as we walk down the aisle. It's Wednesday afternoon, so Dallas and I didn't expect a large crowd. Nonetheless, a good number of our family and close friends are here. This is a much smaller crowd compared to what I saw in the wedding album, but it warms my heart to have them here.

As I get closer to the altar, I see Dallas tearing up. He's not an emotional wreck like he was in our wedding video, but it's still sweet to see him shed a few tears. It makes me feel like this is our first time getting married. I glance at Ashantee and our pastor, comparing them to the wedding album. Before I can remember anything else, however, I get a stabbing pain on the side of my head. It's the same pain I got in the grocery store parking lot that day.

Shaking my head, I decide to stop living in the past and focus on the present. Momma fills in for Daddy, announcing that she gives me away as Dallas reaches for my hand and brings me on the altar with him. After handing Ashantee my bouquet, Dallas and I smile at each other as we hold hands and stare into each other's eyes.

The pastor begins the ceremony, and before long it's time for the vow exchange. Dallas repeats his vows verbatim, looking into my eyes the whole time. I smile when it's my turn.

"Shauntay, repeat after me," the pastor instructs. "I, Shauntay."

"I, Shauntay."

"Take you, Dallas."

"Take you, Dallas."

"To be my lawfully wedded husband."

The sharp pain returns to the side of my head before I open my mouth. The pain is so strong that it causes me to wince and lower my hands.

"You okay?" Dallas asks, securing my hand in his.

Nodding, I say, "To be my lawfully wedded husband."

"To...have...and...to...hold..." The pastor says, causing me to look at him. Why is his speech slowing?

I face Dallas again, and as I open my mouth to repeat the vows, a scene flashes into my mind. It's hard to make sense out of it, but it seems to be from my first wedding. My head hurts the more the memory plays.

"Shauntay," Dallas says, worry written over his face. "What's wrong?"

My head starts spinning, and my vision becomes blurry. I start falling backwards before Dallas catches me.

"Manny!" he says, calling for Ashantee's husband. He's a pediatrician if I remember correctly, but I'm sure Dallas isn't biased toward any medical care right now.

"She has a pulse," Manny says, letting my wrist go.

Someone scoops me up, and from the scent of the cologne, it's Dallas. It hurts too much for me to move, so I just collapse in his arms. I try to open my eyes, but everything is still blurry.

The present day starts fusing with the past. Someone is telling Dallas to take me into a chamber room while my mind is playing a scene of Dallas and me at freshmen orientation. Manny opens my eye and shines a light into it as I'm remembering introducing Dallas to Daddy for the first time.

"Daddy?" I mumble.

That's right. He died, and that's when everything happened. The roller-coaster in my mind finally slows after playing the last eight years of my life in fast-forward.

"Tay," Ashantee frantically calls.

"Yes, Tee?" I say, trying to sit up.

"We should get her to the hospital to make sure she's okay," Manny says.

"I'm fine," I say, slowly opening my eyes.

I see that we're in a room at church. I'm reclined on a sofa with Ashantee, Manny, Momma, the pastor, and Dallas around me.

"How do you feel?" Manny asks. "Can you tell me your name?"

"I'm fine, Manny," I say, pushing the light out of my eyes. "I'm Shauntay Monroe. Now someone tell me what we're doing here and why y'all are all dressed up," I demand before gazing down at my outfit. I gasp before looking at Dallas. My heart starts racing, and I start breathing heavily.

"Easy, Shauntay," Manny instructs, turning my face to him. He asks me a series of questions while checking my pulse every so often. By this time, the pastor has left to inform everyone that there will be a delay, and Ashantee has provided Manny with his medic bag. "She's fine from what I can tell, but I strongly suggest she get checked out at a medical facility," Manny advises.

"Are you okay?" Ashantee asks, coming to my side.

I nod before looking at Dallas. He's been silently staring at me during my examination. "I'm fine," I say, still staring at him. "I remember everything." The lies. The arguments. The unhappiness and the cheating.

"Is there anything you need us to do?" Ashantee asks.

"Can y'all leave Dallas and me alone for a minute?"

A worried look comes across Ashantee and Momma's faces as they stand to leave.

"Hey, Peaches," Dallas says, approaching me when we're alone. "I'm glad your memory's back."

"Are you?" The question leaves my mouth more aggressively than I anticipated.

Dallas winces at my tone before taking a deep breath. "Why wouldn't I be?"

"What's all of this?" I ask, gesturing to his tux and my gown.

"We're getting married again," he answers. I silently stare at him. "Unless your memory returning means you no longer want to."

"I don't know what to think," I whisper. "The last time you and I sat down to discuss something this calmly was with a divorce lawyer."

"Yeah," he says, looking away.

"And I think it's my fault."

Dallas faces me with a raised eyebrow. "What's your fault?"

"The reason our marriage spiraled downward the way it did," I confess, my voice breaking. "I was so heartless and cold after Daddy died. He was gone so suddenly, and in the blink of an eye, so was our son. Three months had gone by since they died, and there was a hole in my heart that wouldn't close. No matter what I tried, I couldn't mend it. I wanted to become someone different, and I wanted something new because every time I looked at you... Every time we talked or touched...I was reminded of everything I lost." Taking a deep breath, I wipe my tears before they can fall. "You did nothing wrong, Dallas. I just felt unworthy of your love," I confess, looking into his eyes.

"Why didn't you share any of this with me, Peaches?" he asks, his voice gentle and welcoming.

I roll my eyes. "I don't know, Dallas. What woman goes to her husband and shares her insecurities? What woman confesses to her husband that she feels like a failure because she couldn't cope with the death of her father and loss of her child? You deserved someone better."

"I'm your best friend, Peaches. If you needed me to show up as your friend and not your husband, then all you had to do was express that. I didn't mind holding you those nights you had to cry yourself to sleep. I didn't mind comforting you as we took down the nursery decorations. What I minded was you putting up a wall between us. What I didn't like was you not wanting me to talk to or touch you. What hurt the most was you telling me to sleep in the guest room and that you want a divorce. I felt blindsided, Shauntay. To me, all of that came out of nowhere, and before I could fix one thing, everything else collapsed."

I take another deep breath. "Brian and I started having an affair after my job's Christmas party two years ago," I confess. Dallas' face hardens. "I tried to break it off...but after a while...anyway, when I found out about your affair, I realized that we were both happy with the choices we made, so there was no point in us sharing a bed, or room, or lives anymore. I assumed you found someone to replace me, and I found someone to be content with, so everyone was happy."

Dallas sighs. "I could never replace you, Shauntay. I won't deny that I had strong feelings for Misty, and based on your messages with Brian, you had strong feelings for him too, but you're still the only woman I want."

"Why'd you do it?" I ask, unable to stop the tears from falling this time. "Why'd you still take care of me? Why didn't you just give up on us? Why didn't you throw it away? You would've been happier."

Dallas removes his handkerchief from his pocket and carefully dabs my face. "When we first got together, I was convinced that I was in a dream. No one else could separate me from my background. People were either scared of me or mocked me for being from Mechanicsville. Others insulted my intelligence because of the high school I went to. Few wanted to hang out with me, let alone date me, claiming that no good could come of a child raised by a single mother in my neighborhood. You looked at me and saw who I am. You didn't care where I came from or what my home life was like. You liked me for me, and for that I fell in love with you. For that, I vowed my heart to you before we even had our first kiss." He caresses my cheek before turning my head so I can look into his eyes. "And I'm willing to do it again."

"But think about—"

"Think about the last four months. Think about our first four years dating, and our first six years married. Is it worth throwing all of that out for two bad years?"

Momma's words from earlier replay in my mind. "No," I answer, crying harder. "I'm so sorry, Dallas. Can you forgive me, please?"

"I've already forgiven you for that," he says, dabbing my face again. "What I won't forgive you for is ruining this makeup before we make it to the honeymoon suite. I need you to keep it together for me, Peaches."

I chuckle. "Making love only made me cry once," I say, smiling at him.

"And I'll make it happen again," he says, standing up and extending his hand to me.

"Okay, Mr. Ten Minutes."

Dallas' eyes widen. "That only happened the first time."

I chuckle. "And I'll make it happen again," I challenge, wrapping my arms around him. Dallas takes me into his arms, but before we can kiss, the chamber's door opens.

"I guess you two are ready to resume the ceremony?" the pastor asks.

Dallas and I laugh before nodding our heads. Dallas returns to the altar, and I reenter from the floor. He helps me onto the altar, and we resume the ceremony where we left off.

"In sickness and in health," the pastor says.

"In sickness and amnesia," I say, causing everyone to laugh.

"Till death do us part."

"Till death do us part," I say, squeezing Dallas' hands.

After the ring ceremony, the pastor says, "I now pronounce you man and wife, again. You may kiss your bride."

I wrap my arms around Dallas's neck as he wraps his around my waist. We kiss, and it's the seal on our renewed journey together. Our family and friends clap, but I don't want to let Dallas go. I don't want this feeling to end.

"I take it you two won't be at the reception," the pastor jokes, which is enough to make Dallas and me part.

Dallas and I hold hands as we head to the fellowship hall for the reception. Rather than a traditional reception, we opted for a meal and wedding cake. We welcomed gifts but didn't require any. Everyone eats, dances, and enjoys themselves.

"I wish I could get a redo on the last two years," I tell Dallas as we head to a hotel later that night.

"The last two years are just a drop in the bucket," he says, taking my hand in his. "It's nothing compared to what's next."

Chapter 15: Dallas Monroe

AUGUST 29,2022

I get every single red light on the way to Shauntay's job. I was supposed to meet her at the doctor's office an hour ago. She went to the doctor a few weeks ago for a final follow-up from her accident. The doctor did a complete exam, ordered blood work, and asked Shauntay to schedule an appointment to review the results.

She texted me when she was on her way back to work, and though she didn't explicitly state it, I know she's upset. If there's one thing Shauntay doesn't like, it's being stood up. I didn't intentionally plan to be late, but my appointment ran longer than anticipated. Before Shauntay left the house for work this morning, she asked if I could meet her at the doctor's office a few minutes before her appointment so we could talk. She didn't give me any other information, so I can't deduce what she wants to talk about.

Things between us have been wonderful since her memory returned. We work through disagreements when they arise, and we've both been faithful. Shauntay returned to work two weeks ago. She hasn't mentioned Brian to me since returning, and I haven't asked, so I can't imagine that's what she wants to talk about.

I turn into her job's parking deck, grab the fast food I bought for her, and hop out of the car. I haven't been to Shauntay's job in years, but after securing a visitor's pass, I take the elevator to the sixth floor and stop at her office as if it's muscle memory. I tap on her office window before opening the door. She folds her arms as she stands and walks to the front of her desk.

"I'm sorry, Peaches," I say, dropping the food on her desk. She rolls her eyes as I hug her. "How did it go?"

"Where were you?" Her tone is soft, but I can tell she's upset.

"I had an appointment that I couldn't miss. I can't wait to tell you about it, but I want you to tell me what's on your mind first."

"It would've been nice to talk to you before seeing the doctor, but now..." she shrugs. "It doesn't even matter."

"Don't do that," I say, shaking my head. "No more walls; you promised."

The morning after the wedding, Shauntay and I flew to Florida for a five-day cruise for our anniversary. While there, she and I shared a lot of things with each other. I shared that one thing that worried me going forward was whether she would lock me out of her feelings again. She promised she never would.

"I wanted to talk to you about my job," she says, taking my hand in hers but not looking into my eyes.

I remain calm while ignoring the thoughts telling me something happened with her and Brian.

"It's been hard getting readjusted to my office life, even though it's the same place I've worked at since graduating from college," she continues. "I was going to ask how you'd feel about me remaining a stay-at-home wife." Shauntay finally meets my gaze then. "I know financially things will be different since I won't be bringing a check home anymore, but if we could've afforded it, then I would've asked to stop working."

"Is that all?" I ask, tightening my grip around her hands. "We can afford it," I assure.

"No, we can't," she says, shaking her head. "Not anymore. I'm going to be making more trips to the doctor in the upcoming months."

I give her a bewildered look. "Why? What's wrong? What did she say?"

"We're having a baby," Shauntay shares, smiling as a few tears fall from her eyes. "I'm about six weeks, and we've set up an appointment to meet with an obstetrician."

"That's wonderful," I say, hugging her. We never talked about trying for another baby, but we didn't take any precautions to ensure we wouldn't conceive either.

"It is, and that's why I can't quit," she says into my shirt. "We won't be able to afford it."

I let her go so I can look into her eyes. "Do you really prefer to be at home?"

She nods. "I enjoyed the free time I had to do whatever I wanted whenever I wanted. I liked waiting for you to come home from work, having an early dinner with you before you left, packing you lunch to make it through your shift, and sending you spicy pictures during your break," she says, causing me to smile. "I also like posting my cooking videos online. Now we only see each other in passing except on the weekends. I miss having quality time with you."

"Then quit," I tell her.

Her eyes widen. "I can't quit, baby. I don't want us living from check to check."

"We won't be. I'm late because I had a job interview with Taylor Enterprise today."

Shauntay gasps. "I didn't even know you were still applying to other jobs."

"I began reapplying to jobs in March. We both know that Taylor Enterprise is a prestigious company. I never expected to hear back from them, so when they called and asked if I could come in for an interview, I didn't think twice about going."

"How did it go?"

"They're opening a new marketing department, and though I haven't been in the field for a few years, after explaining my qualifications and skills, they offered me a position as a team lead."

"Team lead?!" Shauntay exclaims.

"I was a team lead before my prior company went bankrupt. I'll have a six-month training process starting next month. During that time, they'll assess my skills to see if I'm still qualified for that role. During training, they'll start me off at $65,000, and if I meet their expectations, then my salary will increase to $70,000, which is the standard pay for someone in my position. Afterward, I have the potential for yearly raises."

"That's fantastic news!" she says, hugging me again.

"So, you can quit, Peaches," I say, holding her and kissing her forehead. "You can give a two-week notice, finish out the month, or leave right now."

"You can't be serious, baby," she chuckles as she lets me go. "Pack up my belongings now and quit?"

"I'll help if you want," I say, grabbing a random stack of paper.

"My job's been nice to me during my leave, so I'll finish out the month," she says, still amused. "But thank you for taking this chance on me."

"What chance?" I ask, puzzled.

"The chance to strive to be the best wife I can be to you," she says, smiling.

"You already were the best wife," I say, pulling her to me. "And soon you'll be the best mom."

She throws her arms around my neck and kisses me. As I wrap my arms around her waist and hold her tightly, I can't help but feel at home.

THE END

www.ingramcontent.com/pod-product-compliance
Lightning Source LLC
LaVergne TN
LVHW090615110826
845146LV00001B/399